SHADOWS ON A SWORD

THE SECOND BOOK OF THE CRUSADES

KARLEEN BRADFORD

HarperCollins*PublishersLtd*

For Rachna Gilmore, Jan Andrews, Caroline Parry
and my editor, Marie Campbell, who all helped me to
chip away the stone and find the story

http://www.harpercollins.com/canada

First published in hardcover by HarperCollins Publishers Ltd: 1996
First HarperCollins Publishers Ltd mass market edition: 1997

Canadian Cataloguing in Publication Data

Bradford, Karleen
    Shadows on a sword : the second book of the Crusades

ISBN 0-00-648054-3

I. Title.

PS8553.R217S53   jC813'.54   C95-933326-6
PZ7.B73Sh

97 98 99 ❖ OPM 10 9 8 7 6 5 4 3 2 1

Printed and bound in the United States

THE FIRST CRUSADE 1096–1099

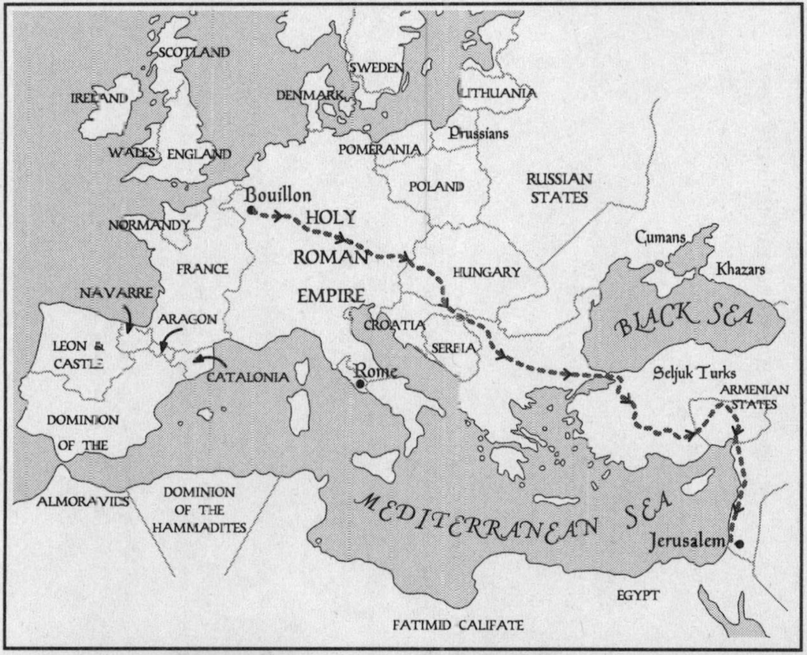

Prologue

In the year 1096, Pope Urban II responded to the Byzantine Emperor Alexius's plea for help in recapturing the lands that the Seljuk Turks had conquered. The pope called for a holy crusade to liberate Jerusalem.

A monk named Peter, also called Peter the Hermit, set out in April of that year from Cologne, Germany, with over twenty-thousand followers. This People's Crusade, as it came to be called, was destined to end in disaster. Peter's motley band included only a few nobles trained in the art of war, and their foot soldiers. For the most part, it was made up of pilgrims anxious to liberate Jerusalem, and criminals released from prisons upon the pope's promise of pardon for the sins of all who took part in the crusade.

The People's Crusade swept across Germany, Hungary and Serbia on its way to Constantinople in Turkey. The travelers soon ran out of supplies and resorted to looting and pillaging villages as they passed. Other small groups of crusaders were also making their way across Europe and they, too, were causing havoc. Villagers, at first supportive, became fearful and resentful of these roving bands. Battles broke out between Peter's followers and the soldiers and villagers of the towns through which they journeyed. In the town of Semlin, in Hungary, which had already suffered at the hands of crusaders following Walter Sans-Avoir, Peter's followers killed four thousand people after a dispute over a pair of shoes. A final ambush by the Turkish army, just outside Constantinople, ended Peter's hopes. He settled down to wait, with the few survivors, for the First Crusade to catch up with them.

The First Crusade was composed of some of the greatest princes and knights in Germany, France and Normandy, with their well-trained armies and their followers. One of the most noble and respected leaders of this expedition was Godfrey of Bouillon, who set out in August of the same year to meet up with the others in Constantinople and, with them, march on to Jerusalem.

One

Theo raised his eyes. The sword flashed in the sunlight above him. His hands clenched into fists, and he pressed them hard against his thighs as he knelt on the sweet-smelling grass of the meadow. He willed himself to stay absolutely still, his face to remain impassive, but a singing excitement rising inside him threatened to burst out at any moment.

A touch on his shoulder; a light blow to the cheek.

"Rise, Theobald." Count Garnier's deep, slightly husky voice rang out.

Theo stood. All of the count's men were there to witness the knighting of a boy they had known for most of his life. The count lowered the sword and held it out before him, flat on the palms of his hands. The priest, robes stirring in the slight summer breeze, made the sign of the cross over it.

"Bless this sword, Holy Lord, Almighty Father, Eternal God . . ." His words resounded so that all assembled could hear.

The count then fastened the sword around Theo's waist. His movements were deliberate, solemn. Theo forced himself to stare straight ahead, even though his eyes squinted in the sun's glare. He was determined that his knees should not tremble as the count's oldest squire, Hugh, knelt to fasten gleaming new spurs to Theo's soft leather boots.

Hugh finished and stepped back. He caught Theo's gaze and held it for a moment. He had been Theo's instructor throughout all the years of his youth, and his eyes shone with pride. Theo grasped the pommel of his sword. It felt cold in spite of the heat of this late summer's day. He took a deep breath and, with a quick, determined movement, unsheathed the weapon and held it high. Cheers shattered the silence.

Three times Theo brandished the sword, and then he returned it to its scabbard. The cheers redoubled. The count's face broke into a smile, cracking the weather-beaten skin into unfamiliar creases around his eyes and mouth. Now, finally, Theo relaxed. He let out the breath he had been holding and stepped forward to receive his foster father's embrace. His own smile, wide as it was, was still only a shadow of the great happiness that welled up within him. He was a knight. At last.

Overflowing with eagerness to fulfill his duties, to prove his faith and courage, he had stayed alone at prayer all the night before in the church, dedicating himself to God and to his master. Earlier this morning, he had attended mass amid the smoke of incense and the glow of candles. And now it was over. He was a knight, pledged into his foster father Count Garnier's service. Although he had as yet seen only seventeen summers, the war that loomed ahead of them promised to be the biggest, the grandest yet, and the count had need of him.

I will not fail him, Theo vowed. He had been sent to the count by his father as a boy of seven years, according to the custom of the time. He had served him first as page, then as squire. Now he could take his place beside him as knight. His head swam with the heat of the day and with magnificent visions— visions of the battle to come, and of the joy of fighting side by side with his master for the glory of God. They would be invincible, he was certain of it.

They were assembling and making ready for a holy crusade to liberate Jerusalem from the heathen. Pope Urban himself had called for it, and the nobles of all the Frankish and German lands were gathering. In less than two weeks—just after the Feast of the Assumption—they would set out. It would be the greatest war the world had ever seen, and he would be a part of it. When Jerusalem was Christian again, he would be there. He would be among the heroes who set it free.

A trumpet sounded, closely followed by another.

"Master?" A low voice brought him back. "Your horse, if you are ready?"

Theo whipped around. His groom, William, stood waiting, eyes averted as always. To Theo's annoyance, the man never seemed to look him in the eye. William had been sent to him by his father, however, and Theo could not reject this generosity. His father had also presented him with the sword and the spurs, the embossed shield, the metal-ringed leather tunic and helmet that weighed so heavily upon him, and the magnificent warhorse whose reins the groom now held. Fine gifts, but Theo's mouth quirked down, a momentary pall cast over his triumph. His father had provided for him well, but Theo knew that, in return, he was expected to acknowledge that he would receive nothing else. The manor, the land—all would go to an elder brother he scarcely knew. It was up to Theo now to provide for himself for the rest of his life. He forced a civil reply to the groom.

"My thanks, William," he said.

He is a very good groom, he reminded himself. I should not be so ungrateful.

At the servant's side, saddled and caparisoned in a crimson blanket, the massive warhorse snorted, stamping his enormous hooves and tossing his mane as if to jerk the reins out of the man's hands. The groom gave the horse a light impatient slap. The animal's eyes rolled wickedly.

Theo raised his eyebrows slightly. Good groom or not, William treated the charger in a way that didn't seem quite right. Theo had not yet had a chance to ride the horse, but he had spent a few minutes with him the day before. Enough time to realize that the shining, roan-colored warhorse was worthy of respect—and also had a healthy liking for turnips.

There was a sudden cry from William, then a quickly suppressed curse. Theo saw that the charger had shifted his weight and planted one plate-sized hoof on the groom's foot. William was pushing at the animal's haunches, trying vainly to move him. The groom's face was contorted with pain. The horse stared into the distance as if totally unaware of the havoc he was causing; then, with a heaving sigh, he casually shifted his weight again. William leaped back. He hopped on one leg and raised the other foot to massage it, glaring all the while at the backside of the charger. Theo took the reins from him and hid a smile. Yes, this horse was definitely an animal to be reckoned with.

More trumpets. Theo looked out at the meadow in front of him. Ringed with the ancient, towering trees of the Ardennes forest, the fields lay flat, then sloped gently upward. Count Garnier's castle was situated at the top of the rise, silhouetted black against the deep blue sky. Today, the count was hosting the last great tournament planned before their departure. The vast green expanse between Theo and the castle on the hill was dotted with brightly colored tents and flying streamers. Seats had been arranged for the ladies and their retinues. Knights with their warhorses, squires and grooms gathered in knots around the edges of the jousting grounds.

A commotion at the far end announced the arrival of Godfrey of Bouillon, Duke of Lower Lorraine. One of the greatest and most honorable princes in all of France, he would lead Count Garnier and the other Lorrainers on this crusade.

Godfrey rode up to where the count and Theo stood. His charger was a dapple gray, but so hung with gold and jewelled trappings that little could be seen of its original hide. The sunlight glinted off all the adornments in dazzling shafts. The duke saluted Garnier, and inclined his head toward Theo.

"A noble knight you make," he said. "I shall be honored to number you among my party."

Theo dropped to one knee. "It is my honor to serve you, my lord." His blood was pounding through his veins so hard that the sound of it in his ears blocked out everything else. He felt it rush to his cheeks and did not dare raise his face. He had seen the duke from afar, and knew the stories, almost legends, of his bravery, but this was the first time Godfrey had ever spoken to him.

Godfrey gestured to Theo to rise, then rode on. He drew up before the largest of all the tents that dotted this end of the field. His men ranged themselves behind him, pennants snapping in the quickening wind. His trumpeter blew a long, sharp blast—the signal for the tournament to begin.

Theo snatched the reins from William's hands and mounted quickly. Count Garnier was already riding toward their allotted spot, the rest of his men following. The count would be among the early jousters, Theo knew. He turned his horse to follow him. At the kick of Theo's spurs, the charger rolled his eyes back to look at his new master, then strode majestically and unhurriedly forward, as if the decision had been his own.

"You do have a mind of your own, don't you?" Theo said. Ears set far apart on either side of the horse's broad head twitched back at the sound of his voice. "And a noble Roman nose. A noble Roman nose like that deserves a noble Roman name. I shall call you Centurion." The feel of the wide body between his knees was reassuring, and the strong horse smell enveloped him.

How will you fare in the lists, my friend? Theo wondered. His very life would depend on this horse. Then—how will *we* fare? The thought made him catch his breath. As the youngest and newest of all the knights, his turn would come late in the day, if it came at all, but suddenly there was a nervous sickness in his stomach and a sour taste in his mouth. In practice with the count's other knights, all well known to him, Theo had shown promise and done well, but today . . . Today he would be up against strangers, all formidable foes. He fought to breathe normally. He would be going into battle, real battle, very soon—a mere jousting tournament should not be cause for fright. But jousting tournaments were not to be taken lightly.

"A knight cannot shine in war if he has not prepared for battle in tournaments." The words of the count's old squire, Hugh, echoed in Theo's mind. Hugh had trained Theo well. "See your own blood flow, feel your own teeth crack with a well-aimed blow, that's what you need, my young friend." He had seen to it that Theo had experienced some of that pain, and Theo winced with the memory. Many of the tournaments Theo had taken part in had been, in fact, little more than undisciplined brawls. Men were injured frequently, and sometimes even killed. Godfrey, however, would have none of that. He had established rules and insisted on them being carried out strictly.

"We have many battles to come," he had said. "I will not have my men die needlessly beforehand."

Yet, as Theo watched, the very first bout brought death. Count Reginald, one of Godfrey's own noblemen, caught his opponent squarely on the shield with his long, blunt-nosed lance, and unhorsed him.

The warhorse bolted. With his foot caught in the stirrup, the knight was dragged the length of the field before grooms were able to run out and get the horse back under control. The knight lay still on the ground. His own two squires carried him off.

"One who will not be with us on our journey, I fear," Count Garnier said. His voice was tight. His own bout was next.

Theo willed his mind to go blank, to shut the fear out. He had seen death before. He dug his fingers into the thick, wiry gray mane of his warhorse. Centurion shuddered, and shifted nervously.

A superb horseman, the count defeated his opponent easily. The others of his house did equally well. By the time it finally came to Theo's turn, the nervousness in his stomach had turned into a knot of pain. He swallowed hard as he tightened up the reins. The sour taste was worse. He settled his shield into his left shoulder, and received his lance from his groom. Across the field from him, another knight was making his preparations. Sweat poured into Theo's eyes, but even with a free hand, he would not have been able to reach under the metal nose and forehead guard of his helmet. He blinked. The field in front of him blurred. A spot between his shoulder blades began to itch. Trumpets blared out. Centurion carved a deep half-moon into the green turf with one anxious stamp of a hoof. Theo clenched his right fist around the shaft of his lance, balanced the weight of it, and spurred the warhorse on.

"Now, Centurion!" he cried.

Centurion reacted with an explosion of movement unbelievable in an animal so immense. Theo found himself hurtling toward his opponent. The two horses crossed, careening within inches of each other. Great gobs of grass and earth flew into the air with the impact of the animals' hooves. Theo felt his lance strike the other's shield, then glance off. At the same instant, his opponent's lance struck Theo's shield with such force that, for a moment, Theo lost his balance. He tottered, almost lost his seat, then gripped desperately with his knees and managed to remain in the saddle. He was already past the other knight and galloping toward the far end of the field.

He pulled back hard on the reins, forcing Centurion into a tight turn. The charger snorted, flecks of foam flying from his mouth. Theo collected himself and quieted the horse. He settled his shield, renewed his grip on his lance. Across the field, his opponent was preparing himself again as well. They turned their chargers and faced each other. The warhorses, frantic with excitement now, tore at their bridles and ripped the ground with their hooves.

The signal sounded once more. Theo's training took over. Aim low, in at the side, under the shoulder. Get under the shield! The horses raced toward each other, sweat-soaked withers colliding. This time, his opponent's lance missed completely, but Theo's found its mark with a jar that sent splinters of pain up his arm and into his shoulder. He held fast. The other knight let out a cry and flew out of his saddle. Theo twisted to look, even as he pulled at Centurion's bridle to swing him around again. A clean fall. The other knight was already on his knees. A surge of triumph flooded through Theo. He had won!

As Theo checked Centurion and looked down at his fallen opponent, the other looked back up at him. Their eyes locked. The knight was young, probably not much older than Theo. What could be seen of his face was purple with rage and humiliation. Theo lifted his lance in a salute.

"Well fought," he began.

The other spat onto the ground.

The trumpets sounded for the last time, signaling the end of the tournament. Theo wheeled Centurion away. If the knight was so ill-mannered, that was his concern. He, Theo, would not have been so ungracious in defeat. Still, the triumph he had felt was lessened somewhat. He galloped back to the count's enclosure. When he reached it, he leaped from his horse and threw the reins to William. He tore off the confining helmet, tossed it to the ground and swept his short hair back out of his eyes. When dry, his hair was light, almost corn-colored, but now it clung to his scalp, dark with sweat. The count's men surrounded him. They thumped him on the back and pummeled him with affection until the breath was nearly knocked out of him. The squire, Hugh, shook his hand, dropped it, then reached to shake it again.

"A fine showing for your first joust as a knight, my young lord. A *fine* showing." His face shone ruddy with pleasure.

Theo glowed at the praise. My first victory, he thought. And there will be many others. So many others! Real victories against real enemies. The memory of his opponent's churlish behavior vanished from his mind. Of what importance was that? I've proven myself, Theo thought. And in front of my foster father and the duke himself.

"Come, Theo," Count Garnier called from outside the circle of men. "You have earned the right to your feast." He waved Theo forward and led the way across the field back toward the castle.

Around Theo, the whole meadow was a mass of moving color, converging in a noisy, babbling horde upon the castle grounds. Long trestle tables had been set up in the fields, and servants were heaping them high with food. Theo had passed through the great stone-floored kitchens early that morning and had seen the maids already hard at work, cauldrons boiling over the fires. Small boys had been turning spits on which whole carcasses of deer and boar roasted; pigeons and other birds by the hundreds had been tipped out of gamebags in sticky, bleeding heaps onto the floors. The heavy, oily smell of roasting and boiling meat had been overwhelming, almost nauseating then. Now, however, the smells awakened a

12

voracious appetite within him. He had not eaten since the evening before. He strode eagerly to the feast, congratulating and receiving congratulations from everyone he met.

An arm suddenly landed on his shoulders. Startled, he looked up.

"That was bravely done!" A young knight fell into step beside him. He was dark of complexion, and thick curling brown hair obscured his eyes. "Guy will not soon forgive you for that embarrassment."

"Guy?" Theo stammered, taken by surprise.

"My cousin. He rides with me, but has no fondness for me. He has no fondness for any man, I think. He never forgives a slight. I am Amalric," he added. "Foster son to Godfrey, Duke of Lorraine."

"I am Theobald—"

"Foster son of Count Garnier. We go together on this grand adventure." Amalric's eyes shone and he tossed his head, almost in the manner of Theo's charger. "We are blessed, are we not? Surely this will be the greatest quest known to man."

"So it will," Theo answered eagerly. There was an enthusiasm and openness about the young knight that attracted him immediately. He matched his stride to Amalric's.

"Feast at our table. I would like to know you better." Amalric urged Theo toward several trestles set up at the very head of the field. Godfrey was already seated at the topmost table, surrounded by knights and ladies. The women's flowing, colorful gowns fluttered in the wind like butterflies in a meadow of wildflowers. Children were there, too.

"Gladly," Theo assented. He raised his voice and called out to Count Garnier. "My lord?"

The count stopped and looked back.

"Will you excuse me? I would go with Amalric."

The count recognized the young knight. He bowed to Amalric, and smiled at Theo. "Certainly. Come to me later, son," he answered.

Theo followed Amalric.

"Gentlemen, meet Theobald, who disported himself with such glory today!" Amalric cried, as they took their places at a table groaning with food.

At these words, a tall man at the far end leaped to his feet.

"Can he not sup with his own kind, then?" he growled, the words already slurred with wine. "I fancy a better sort to share my food with." With that, he turned his back and headed for another table. In the instant the man had glared at him, Theo had recognized his adversary.

Amalric laughed. "Guy is his usual self, I see. By my life, it was sweet to see you unhorse him today. There are not many who can. And to be bested by such a young, untried boy!" He threw back his head and his laughter turned into a bellow of joy.

The others at the table joined in and made room for Theo. Theo hesitated. Boy he might be, and the worn look of Amalric's mail and tunic showed him to be a more seasoned warrior, but Amalric was not that much older than Theo and his words grated. He almost decided to return to Count Garnier's men, but the warmth of the welcome from all sides overcame his misgivings. And to be singled out by the foster son of Godfrey himself was an honor. Jokes flew as the platters of meat were handed around. Theo's cup was filled with wine; the strong liquid warmed and relaxed him. He was soon laughing with the rest and comfortably at ease in his place beside Amalric.

When the first pangs of his hunger had been assuaged, he pushed back from the table, threw a bone to the hounds fighting in the grass beneath their feet, and looked around. His gaze was drawn to Godfrey's table. This was the first time he had had a chance to observe the famous Duke of Lower Lorraine closely. Godfrey lounged carelessly in his seat, laughing across at another knight. He was tall and massively built, his head and shoulders towering over the others around him. His hair was fair and cut longer than most. Disheveled now after the activity of the day, it hung almost to his shoulders. He had an air of complete confidence. Theo could believe that the tales told of his courage and nobility had not been exaggerated.

He let his glance travel to the others at the table. On one side of the duke sat a lady, and beside her two children. His family, Theo surmised. They would be accompanying the duke on this crusade. On the other side was a dark, wolfish-looking man, with a proud and haughty air. His black eyes stood out from a pale, almost startlingly white face. They moved ceaselessly, suspiciously, even as he held himself taut and almost immobile.

"Baldwin, younger brother to Godfrey," Amalric said beside Theo, following his gaze. "Not a bit like the duke, though. Destined for the church he was, and not allotted any of the family estates. Seems he didn't have the temperament for a churchman, however. Whether he left the church, or the church left him, no one really knows, but here he is now, taking his brother's charity. You'd never know it by his manner, though. You'd think *he* was the great lord, the way he carries himself. They say he's more interested in making his fortune in the east than in the holy quest."

A minstrel group struck up a few notes, and Amalric turned away, instantly distracted.

"Music! Now we shall have some fun!"

Theo remained staring at Baldwin. At his side sat a stout, rather homely woman, eating steadily. Baldwin seemed to pay her no attention at all. His wife, Theo guessed. Beside her sat a line of three children, and beyond them a girl—a girl with thick black hair that streamed down her back and over her shoulders in a mass of undisciplined curls. Unlike the other women at the table, she was dressed in rough, plain-colored homespun. As Theo watched, one of the boys pinched the other and an angry cry rang out. Their mother, her attention focused on the dripping joint she held in her grease-covered hand, gave them barely a glance, but the girl was quick to administer a sharp slap to the aggressor, who then set up a wail of his own.

The girl glanced up and caught Theo's eyes. She stared back at him for one long moment, defiant. Then she turned away.

"Theo!"

With a start, Theo realized Amalric was elbowing him in the ribs. The others were laughing at something he had missed.

"Your pardon?" Theo said quickly. The conversation swirled around him again, but he did not hear. His mind was full of the most wondrous dark, bright eyes he had ever seen in his life.

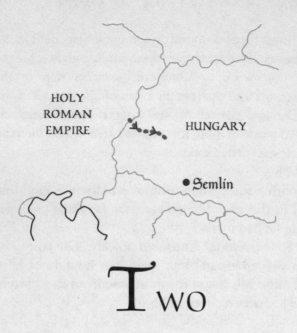

HOLY
ROMAN
EMPIRE

HUNGARY

• Semlin

T WO

"K ing Coloman keeps us waiting still! It is eight days now since Lord Godfrey sent to him for permission to cross his lands!" Amalric's face was flushed and dark, his eyes angry.

"Perhaps he has had a stomach-full of crusaders," Theo answered. In the two months since the crusade had set out from the Frankish lands, Theo had come to know Amalric well.

He's in one of his moods, Theo thought. Almaric was as quick to anger as he was to enthusiasm.

Sometimes it was hard to keep up with him.

Nonetheless, Theo could understand Amalric's impatience. He remembered how they had set out, with such glory, pomp and fanfare. Hundreds of knights had assembled and ridden forth through the dim and leafy forest of the Ardennes in the early morning mists, chain mail gleaming, pennants flying, chargers bedecked in glowing color. Theo had never seen such an assemblage. They had been followed by all their retinue: wives and children in gaily painted wagons and litters, squires and grooms. Behind them, the archers and the foot soldiers, straight-backed, with their long-handled, spear-pointed halberds massed in unswerving, gleaming lines. Behind them, the pilgrims, on foot, on donkeys, in carts—all yearning to make their vows at the Church of the Holy Sepulchre in Jerusalem. A never-ending river of people, it seemed to Theo. Dogs barked and ran to and fro, cattle lowed and bellowed. Chickens and geese added their cackles and shrieks to the cacophony. It was a festive, almost delirious procession, and no one could resist being caught up in the spirit of it. This gathering had much more the look of celebration than of war. But now, it had been brought to a halt here at the frontiers of Hungary.

"He *must* help us. We are God's army." Amalric was vehement in his indignation.

"So is Peter the Hermit's band, and look what they did."

"Pah! Rabble! That's all his followers are. Criminals and murderers. The dregs of the prisons. Hardly a nobleman among the lot."

"Not so—there are noblemen, and honest pilgrims, as well. Yet they sacked Semlin—a Christian city! I can understand the king's reluctance to admit us. He has heard the tales, too, of the murder of the Jews along the Rhine. I wonder not that he fears us." Theo's voice was heavy. At first, he had not believed the stories of the massacres of the Jews by bands of crusaders in Trier and Mainz and other cities along the German rivers. And then had come news that Count Gottschalk's army had been massacred in its turn by the Hungarians, after the count's men had looted several villages and killed many of the peasants. A young Hungarian boy had been impaled by the crusaders, it was said, and left as a challenge to the Hungarian army. Theo could not bear to think of it. This was not the way the holiest of all wars was to be carried out.

"The villagers refused them food. The crusaders were in need . . ." Amalric's voice trailed off. The tales had been too full of horror. Even he, with all his enthusiasm, could find no excuses.

They were camped on wide fields beside the Danube River. When they had arrived, the fields had been rich with the late fall harvest. After eight days, however, any crops not pulled up by the crusaders had been trampled into garbage. Theo looked around. It was a dispiriting sight. As far as he could see were tents and makeshift shelters. People gathered by small fires, beginning to prepare their evening meal. Pennants flew as usual in the brisk October breeze, but somehow they did not impart any air of gaiety. The camp was unusually quiet. Here and there children's voices broke the stillness, and dogs barked defiance at one another and the world in general, but over all hung an air of listlessness and waiting. The weather had been warm for this time of year; the stink of the camp permeated everything.

At first, curious villagers had ventured out to see this incredible army, some even carrying gifts of food and clothing, but none had appeared for the last two days. Food was running short, tempers were rising. Fights broke out.

Suddenly, Theo could bear it no longer. "I must return to the count," he said.

"Will you meet me here tomorrow morning?" Amalric asked. "I would try my hand at hunting for a few birds in the woods. We're not overly short of food yet, but anything extra for the pot is welcome."

"Gladly." Theo felt a twinge of guilt as he spoke. Count Garnier had laid in wagonloads of supplies, and his people, like Godfrey's, were suffering no want of food as yet; but every evening, as Theo wandered through the camp, he could not help but realize that the mass of common people were beginning to suffer. Now, as he turned back toward his tent, he deliberately chose a path away from the river's edge where most were settled.

Baldwin's tents also lay in this direction. There was, perhaps, a chance he might see the girl who was nursemaid to Baldwin's children—the girl who had intrigued him so the day of the tournament. He had found out from Amalric that her name was Emma, but when Amalric realized how curious Theo was about her and began to tease him, Theo had not mentioned her again. Amalric could be merciless when he had the bit between his teeth, and, friend or not, was not above humiliating Theo completely before the other knights. He had done it before to other luckless young men.

Theo had seen Emma two or three times in the distance, but always with the children or with Baldwin's lady, Godvere. Now, as he drew near to their camp, he heard Godvere's angry voice. The sound of a slap followed. The bushes in front of him parted, and a figure pushed through. As if his thoughts had suddenly taken shape, Emma appeared.

The girl was wiping her eyes as she emerged, but at the sight of Theo her hand dropped. She swung her heavy hair away from her face with a toss of her head and faced Theo warily. A welt was rising on one cheek.

"Is anything amiss?" The words sprang from Theo's lips before he had time to think.

"Amiss? No more than usual." The girl's voice shook. Theo could see the effort she was making to steady it. She eyed him with distrust and took a step back toward her encampment.

"No—stay!" Again, Theo spoke impulsively. "I . . . I saw you at the feast," he added. To his chagrin, he realized he was stuttering.

"And I saw you looking at me," Emma replied. There was a hint of scorn now in her tone, as if she were well used to being stared at by rude young knights.

With her black hair billowing around her face, her dark eyes and her flushed cheeks, Theo thought her quite the most beautiful woman he had ever seen. He could well imagine men staring at her.

"Your pardon. I did not mean to discomfort you."

"You did not. I am not that easily discomforted."

Theo could well imagine that, also.

"You are nursemaid to Lady Godvere's children?" he asked, trying desperately for some way to reassure her, to keep her from leaving. He was careful to make no move toward her.

"I am. And you—you are foster son to Count Garnier, are you not?"

Theo looked at her in surprise. How did she know that? Had she, by any chance, been making enquiries about him?

"Amalric said so," she added, squelching his hope that she might be as interested in him as he was in her. "He is much about our camp and has spoken of you. I could not help but overhear."

"Oh," was all that Theo could manage.

Emma reached out to break a twig off a bush. She started to peel the bark from it with long, slender

23

fingers. In the gathering dusk, Theo could see that her hands were work-hardened, but fine. She looked at him for a long moment, and bit her lip. Then she tossed the twig away with a decisive movement, as if she had made up her mind about him and concluded there was nothing to fear from this young knight after all. Her face brightened.

"This is a truly wonderful crusade we're on, isn't it?"

"It is," Theo agreed, still treading carefully.

"I wish I were a man. I wish I could fight. I do so envy you!"

"Women cannot fight." The words came out more stiffly than he had intended.

"Oh, I know women can't fight," she said, tossing her hair back again in a movement that completely bewitched him. "Still," she went on, "I can wish for anything I want, can't I? What about you? What will you do after we free Jerusalem?"

The question brought Theo up short. He had never given the matter any thought at all. The crusade alone had filled his mind—the reconquering of Jerusalem. "I shall serve my lord, Count Garnier," he said finally, stuttering again. "What else? He is my father now, and he has no other family but me."

"But will you stay in the Holy Land? They say you will all be given land, houses, riches. They say there are treasures beyond compare to be had there. But perhaps you have even more waiting for you back home?"

"No. No, that I certainly do not have. There is nothing waiting for me back home."

"No girl mooning at the stars and praying at night high upon the battlements of her castle for your safe return?"

Theo bristled. He liked it not that she should take that tone with him. He was not such a callow youth. There had been many girls. He was not that inexperienced. He scowled.

"There is nothing for me to return to," he repeated.

Emma ignored the scowl and smiled. "Then you'll probably stay as well." She looked as if the thought pleased her. Theo's fur settled back down. "It will be exciting, living in a new land, won't it? They say it is very different from our old countries. No poverty, no disease. Wealth and good living for all. I can hardly wait."

"It is probably not all of that," Theo said. "And we must fight for it first." He tried to sound cautious, but her words had chased away his misgivings and reawoken his enthusiasm. How fortunate he was that he was a man and not a mere woman, that he would be able to fight. And had he not shown his mettle in the tournaments? He was ready to go to battle for the glory of God—wealth meant nothing to him. Fighting God's war was what was important—doing God's will. And the battle would be magnificent, he had no doubt of it.

A voice clamored.

"Emma! Emma! Come here at once. Where are you?"

Emma grimaced. "My lady Godvere's gentle summons. I must go." She gave an irritated toss of her head, then smiled before turning to make her way back through the bushes.

Theo stood, looking at the spot where she had disappeared. He could almost believe he had imagined the whole encounter.

† † †

Amalric was striding back and forth when Theo arrived at their meeting place the next morning, just as the first birds began to sing. The rising sun had melted the early morning mists over the fields where the crusaders were encamped, but here, at the edge of the forest, the haze still swirled heavily around them. The air smelled damp, redolent with earth and decaying vegetation. The shadows were deep.

"We are leaving!" Amalric burst out as soon as Theo was within hearing distance. "Coloman has given his permission! We leave tomorrow at sunrise."

"How do you know? When did you hear?" Half asleep still and missing the warmth of his pallet, Theo was slow to react.

"The duke has just come back from King Coloman's court. It seems he made a good impression and managed to convince the king that we are different from the rabble that has preceded us. The word is being passed around the camp now," Amalric said. "We have no time for hunting, we must get ready to move. Besides, the king has agreed to give us all the supplies and provisions we need."

"That is wonderful news indeed," Theo answered. Wide awake now, his excitement rose to match Amalric's. "I wonder what swayed his mind?"

"Well, we are to accept a guard of the king's soldiers while we are crossing his lands. The duke had to give his pledge that there would be no lawlessness. He will call a gathering this afternoon, before the evening mass. He has threatened to kill any man who so much as steals a chicken."

"Then we are on our way!"

"On our way, and nothing can stop us now. We are to march to Constantinople, to the city of the Byzantine Emperor Alexius, and there wait for the other great princes and their entourages to join us. And then . . . Jerusalem!"

"Jerusalem." Theo almost whispered the word. He tried to picture the holy city, but could not. The name itself filled him with awe. He would walk in the footsteps of Christ. He would climb the very hills, follow the very paths His feet had trod . . .

"There is one other condition for our free passage, however."

At first, the words did not even register.

"We must leave hostages with the king."

Finally, Theo heard.

"Hostages? Who?"

"Baldwin and all his family. They are to remain with King Coloman until we are beyond the far borders of Hungary to ensure that we do no harm."

"All his family? Children, too?"

"Yes. There is no cause to fear for them, though. Our men will behave, Godfrey will see to that. No one would dare go against his will. Not that Baldwin would be any great loss, I warrant."

Emma! She would be left here as hostage while they marched on. Theo whirled around.

"Theo! Where are you going?"

He ignored Amalric's cry and dashed back. Early though it was, the camp was in turmoil when he reached it; word had spread that they were to move out the next day. He fought his way through a crowd of people. A dog nipped at his heels; he kicked at it, almost ran into a dying campfire, skirted it and ran on, heading for the outskirts where Baldwin's tents had been. They were already gone. Trampled grass and crumpled refuse were the only signs of where they had stood.

Theo stared at the abandoned camp. There was nothing he could do—nothing but hope that Godfrey could keep his knights and people in order as they marched through Hungary.

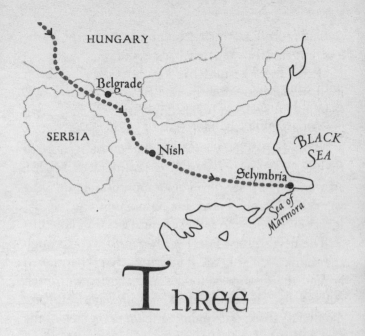

Three

Theo rode with his foster father, or with Amalric, as they followed the river down through Coloman's kingdom. He marveled at the wide fields along the banks of the Danube River. Most of the crops had been harvested, and the level land made the traveling easier than it had been in the narrow defiles and hills along the Rhine and Neckar rivers in Germany. It was still far into the night, however, before he saw the last pilgrims straggle in to make camp at the end of each day.

One morning, Amalric caught up to him, breathless, just shortly after they had set out.

"Peter the Hermit's band of crusaders has been trapped and massacred by the Turks!" he called out, reigning his horse in beside Theo's.

"Where?" Theo asked. "What has happened?"

"At a place called Civetot on the southern shore of the Sea of Marmora, past Constantinople," Amalric answered. He paused to gulp a mouthful of air, then went on. "No one knows for certain, but one tale has it that everyone who followed him has been killed!"

The news spread fast. Fear began to seep through the camp. At night, the mutterings that Theo heard around the fires grew louder and angrier with each passing day. Resentment at the presence of King Coloman's troops surrounding them every step of the way only made things worse.

Theo worried for Emma's safety. It was irrational, he barely knew the girl. She was nothing to him. But if the crusaders' anger boiled over . . . If trouble broke out, he was certain King Coloman would use his hostages in any way necessary to ensure the safety of his people. A small knot of unease sat in the back of his mind and accompanied him wherever he went, whatever he did. Emma was the first thing he thought of in the morning, the last thing in his mind at night before he sank into restless sleep. It amazed him, this preoccupation with her.

In the evenings, after they had made camp, Theo

often met Amalric to hunt. He enjoyed it, and it helped to keep his mind occupied. The Hungarian forests teemed with deer, wild boar and birds of all description. One evening, Amalric met him with further news.

"Peter survived," he said. "My lord Godfrey has just received word. The Hermit was in Constantinople at the time of the attack. A few of his leaders escaped as well, but it seems most of his followers died."

Theo jabbed at the ground with his spear. All appetite for hunting had suddenly deserted him. This news would only make matters worse. At that moment, a shout rang out from the trees ahead of them, and a boar burst into the open, foam flying from its snout, eyes wild and red. It was headed straight for Amalric, who had his back to it.

"Watch out!" Theo realized that Amalric could not possibly turn and defend himself. He braced his feet, raised and threw his spear all in one quick, instinctive movement. The weapon took the animal cleanly behind the shoulder. The force of the boar's charge was checked, but not stopped.

Amalric whirled around. The boar buried one razor-sharp tusk in Amalric's thigh, jerked it out with a tearing, sideways movement of its head, then faltered. Theo pulled his killing dagger from his belt and leaped forward. He was aware of more shouts, but all his attention was on the crazed beast in front of him. Its musky stink filled his nostrils. He yelled. The boar turned and fixed its eyes on Theo. It swerved away from Amalric toward him. Theo raised the dagger high, side-stepped at the last possible moment and plunged the dagger deep into the animal's throat. The boar gave a choking, gurgling snort and dropped to its knees. Its head fell to one side.

"That was *my* animal!"

Theo jerked his gaze away from the dying boar, startled by the shout. The knight he had defeated in the lists, Guy, was standing in front of him, spear held ready as if to throw at him.

"You had no right!"

"No right to defend myself? To defend my friend, your own cousin? Look what *your* animal did to him." Theo shot the words back. The blood-thirst excitement of the danger they had been in, of the killing, roared through him still. He tore the dagger from the boar's body and faced Guy with it. He almost wished the knight would take just one more step toward him.

Guy checked himself. He looked for the first time at Amalric, then turned back to Theo. His face contorted and he threw down his spear.

"You," he snarled, ignoring Amalric. "I might have known it would be you." He spun around and strode back into the woods. His groom, a nervous, bent little man, scurried out and snatched up the spear, eyes averted from Theo and Amalric. Apologies spilled out of him in incoherent fragments.

Theo took a deep breath, willing the storm within him to subside. "Your cousin certainly does not bear you much love," he said finally.

"And less for you, I think," Amalric answered. His words caught in his throat; his mouth twisted in pain.

Theo knelt quickly at his side. Blood was flowing from Amalric's thigh. Theo ripped a piece from the sacking they had been carrying to hold the game, and bound it firmly in place over the wound. Their own grooms, who had been holding their horses in the clearing behind them, came to their aid. Theo helped Amalric to mount.

"We'll get you back to camp," he said. Then, with a sudden mischievous look on his face, he turned to his groom.

"William," he said, "see that the boar is dressed and send it to Guy of Lorraine with my compliments."

Amalric snorted, almost laughing in spite of the pain. "Not a wise thing to do, my friend," he said.

Theo grinned.

† † †

By the end of November, they had reached Semlin. Godfrey had kept order; there had been no trouble. The knights and men of Godfrey's army knew very well that his were not empty threats. Thanks to King Coloman, food and supplies were plentiful, and this generosity helped to offset the resentment his troops caused. Still, Theo and Amalric, whose wound had healed well, hunted in the evenings—for the sport and companionship as well as for the food. Amalric had never actually brought himself to thank Theo for saving his life, but there was a respect in his manner now that made Theo feel he was safe from further teasing or humiliation. He still did not speak of Emma, though. The feelings he had for her were too private to share, even with Amalric. Besides, he had not yet figured out exactly what those feelings were. There would be time enough when he saw her again to try to make sense of them. Amalric, for his part, seemed to have forgotten Baldwin and his entourage entirely.

Theo made a point of keeping out of Guy's way. Guy, in turn, seemed no more inclined to meet Theo. He had never acknowledged the gift of the boar, but Theo doubted that he had eaten it. Thrown it to the dogs, more likely.

They were on the Byzantine frontier now. As soon as they crossed the Save River, they would be out of Hungary, and the hostages would be returned. News had it that Baldwin and all his family were well taken care of, but the knot of unease in Theo's mind still did not loosen. It would only unravel when Emma was free and he could see her again.

Late in the afternoon of their last day in Hungary, Amalric suddenly appeared at Theo's tent. William had just set flint to tinder to start the cookfire to boil the evening stew.

"Don't bother with that," Amalric cried out to Theo as he strode onto the campsite. "I've heard there's a tavern in town that serves a wondrous ale and stew. I shall treat you to a feast."

Theo hesitated for only a moment. The turnips and bit of meat in his pot suddenly looked much less appetizing. Besides, he had not yet had a chance to go into the town, although men had been allowed in, in small groups.

"Done," he agreed. "This stew is all yours, William." He sprang to his feet to accompany Amalric.

As they approached the town of Semlin, Theo looked up at the walls. Here, the arms and clothing of sixteen of Walter Sans-Avoir's men, who had robbed a bazaar, had been hung as a warning to Peter the Hermit's troops. The men had been driven out of the city, naked. It had been a futile warning. The story had been told all over camp before the crusaders had even reached Hungary: how it had only inflamed Peter's followers, and how a dispute over a pair of shoes had escalated into a riot. Peter's men had pillaged the city, leaving four thousand dead. Peter had only managed to save his army by beating a hasty retreat over the Save River, out of the Hungarian kingdom. It was no puzzle why King Coloman had been hesitant to let this new wave of crusaders through.

"I wonder that we would be welcome anywhere within those walls," Theo said.

"A man with money to spend is welcome anywhere," Amalric answered. "The widow who runs the tavern is a friendly sort, they say, and harbors no grudge as long as her customers pay their bills and keep the peace. Besides, she suffered no harm from the crusaders before us. She will make us welcome, be assured of it."

The tavern was overflowing with customers, many of them knights such as themselves, dressed in the rough homespuns of the north. For the most part, these knights were hearty men with simple tastes. They were relaxing after their long march, reveling in the good food and drink, and the warmth. As Theo and Amalric thrust their way among the crowd, a solid wall of smoke and smells hit them. A huge fire at one end of the timbered room blazed, welcome after the early winter chill outside, but contributing its own share to the thick fug within. The room was drowned in noise and loud, raucous laughter. A harried and slightly distraught young maid appeared soon after they had settled themselves at a long trestle table as near the fire as possible. She tucked a few strands of hair behind an ear with one hand, and wiped at the sweat on her forehead with the back of the other. She gave them a wary glance, but smiled nonetheless.

"Your pleasure, my lords?" she asked, her words barely discernible above the clamor.

"Ale, my maid!" Amalric cried. "And food. We hunger for your good victuals." She disappeared, with another smile and a more flirtatious glance at Amalric, and reappeared with tankards of ale. Platters of food soon followed, and within minutes Amalric and Theo were attacking a joint of venison and dipping chunks of coarse, hearty brown bread into a savory-smelling stew. Theo hadn't realized just how hungry he was.

It wasn't until he had filled his belly that he sat back and took a look around. A group in one corner caught his attention. A young woman—a girl, really, probably not even as old as he—was sitting slumped against the wall. A child was sleeping on her lap. The child's long, silver-fair hair was matted and dirty, and hung across her face. The girl's head rested against the timbers behind her; her eyes were closed. Beside her, stretched out on the same bench, with limbs flung out in the loose abandonment of exhaustion, a young man also slept. A dog lay at their feet. They seemed to exist on a silent island of their own, separate from all the hubbub surrounding them.

The landlady bustled up at that moment to enquire if all was well with them.

"Who are those people?" Theo asked.

Her eyes followed his. Her smile dimmed and her brows drew together.

"Those poor young things," she said. "With Peter the Hermit, they were—he that did such terrible things here last summer. There's many who will have nothing to do with them because of it, but I say it was none of their doing, what those soldiers did. They're just poor innocents who got caught up in the whole thing. They say nearly every soul who followed that mad monk was massacred, out there in the heathen lands. They're the first ones we've seen back, and it's a sorry state they're in. If they did do any harm, they've certainly suffered for it." She wiped her hands on her apron. "The wee one will not talk at all, just stares as if her wits are gone completely, and the boy . . . Well, he looks as if he's walking with the devil himself." She quickly made a sign to ward off evil. "The poor girl's done in completely, but she's determined to get them all back to her own land in Germany."

The girl's eyes suddenly opened. She looked straight at Theo, but her gaze was unfocused. Whatever she was seeing was not in that room. She sighed deeply, pulled the ragged cloak she wore more tightly around herself and the child on her lap, and then her lids fell shut again. One hand stroked the child's brow, brushing the hair back out of the little girl's eyes.

"Gave them some soup, I did." The woman's voice broke back in. "They didn't have a copper to pay for it, of course, but they have been on the crusade. It was only Christian charity. The crusade's a wondrous thing, the pope has said so himself—despite some evil men." She crossed herself and bustled off.

"The crusade's a wondrous thing." It did not look as if it had been so wondrous for that small group. Theo stared at them until a nudge from Amalric nearly knocked him off the bench.

"This young wench has a friend who has taken a fancy to you, Theo," he was saying. "Buy her a glass of mead. Show her a Christian knight's courtesy, for mercy's sake."

Theo looked up. The maid who had served them was sitting beside Amalric, who had his arm comfortably around her, and another dark-haired girl was squeezing onto the bench beside them. She laughed and raised her eyes coquettishly to Theo. Their dark brightness gave him a momentary jolt, but they were not the dark eyes that he remembered so well. Suddenly, the miasma of the dark, crowded room sickened him. He couldn't breathe.

"I must get back," he said, rising to his feet so brusquely that his mug of ale almost tipped.

Amalric looked at him in surprise. "So ungracious, my friend? I would not have thought it of you." The ale and the heat in the tavern had brought a flush to his cheeks.

"I'm sorry," Theo blurted out. The others stared at him as he turned and stumbled out.

† † †

The closer they got to the Save River, the more impatient Theo became, but finally, to his relief, they reached its banks. They crossed in all manner of boats and makeshift rafts, amid a chaos of wails and screams from frightened people, and lowing, bleating and neighing from even more terrified animals. The river was calm and not too wide, however, and despite the confusion no lives were lost, not even of livestock.

They reassembled on the other side and made camp outside Belgrade. The town lay silent and deserted. Peter's men had sacked it in celebration of their escape from the Hungarians; the townsfolk had fled and had not returned. Permission was granted to go into the abandoned town, but few took advantage of it. There was nothing left, and the streets had an eerie, desolate appearance. Theo couldn't shake the feeling that they were following in murderous footsteps, rather than progressing in triumph. As soon as they were camped, he hastened to find out if Emma had been released.

"Not yet," his foster father told him when he asked. "Baldwin and his entourage are still with King Coloman. They are being well treated, I hear, and Baldwin is not overly anxious to leave. I expect they'll be with us again soon, though. In the meantime, we will wait." The count gave Theo a curious look, but before he could question him about this sudden interest in Baldwin's affairs, Theo made a hasty excuse and left.

As the days went on and there was still no word of Baldwin's release, Theo's temper became shorter. William learned to avoid him except when absolutely necessary. Theo chafed against the enforced idleness in the camp. He was torn between a desire to get on with the journey, and the need to see Emma and make certain she was all right before they left. Meanwhile, Centurion had discovered the windfalls from the abandoned fruit trees in the orchards near where they were camped. He developed an insatiable appetite for them, plums in particular, and when he had eaten all the ones available on the ground, he devised his own unique way of procuring more of the late-season fruit that still hung on the branches. He ambled heavily up to a tree, leaned his massive weight against it and then bumped it. He was usually rewarded by a rain of fruit that he devoured, pits and all.

It was early in December, and winter was setting in, when they finally left, well rested and reprovisioned. Their way lay along the old Roman road; Centurion's hooves slipped on the ancient stones. Theo rode looking back over his shoulder; Baldwin had not yet rejoined the crusade.

From Belgrade, they would head straight through the Serbian forest to Nish, where the governor, Nicetas, awaited them. He would further replenish their provisions, and provide an escort through the mountains to Sophia and then on to Constantinople. Within a month's time they should be in the fabled city. Stories of its magnificence and grandeur ran the length and breadth of the camp.

"Streets paved with gold," Amalric asserted confidently. "The churches are roofed with it. Every man and woman in the city walks loaded down with jewels."

Theo did not believe half of it, but he knew for certain there were many wonders to be seen. The Hagia Sophia itself was one of the greatest churches in Christendom.

Finally, word came that the hostages had been released. Theo found himself in a frenzy of impatience to see Emma, but it was impossible to seek her out. They were no longer following the great river valley of the Danube, and their way now lay through forest-covered mountains. The marching during the day was difficult and dangerous; at night, the camp was strung out over long stretches of the trail. Halfway to Nish, Governor Nicetas's army met them and gave what aid it could; this time, the crusaders welcomed the escort. Even with the army's help, however, accidents happened daily. Sometimes the slippery paths they followed seemed little better than goat tracks, hanging perilously onto the sides of the mountains. Ponies and horses lost their footing constantly. At one point, the palfrey Theo rode on the trail slipped and almost toppled with him into a chasm so deep that Theo could see only the tops of trees when he looked down into it. Icy streams tumbled from the snow-covered peaks above—higher than any Theo had ever seen before. The travelers were often soaked crossing them. Each day at morning mass, the priest recited prayers for those who had been lost the day before.

At night, Theo bundled himself into his tent, exhausted, usually wet, and always cold, despite his campfire. But the air here in the mountains was so pure that sometimes on clear, dry nights, in spite of the bitter cold, he rolled himself into his cloak and slept out in the open next to his fire. He liked to lie and look heavenward. Never before had he paid any attention to the stars, but here he spent hours studying them. He could lose himself in the vastness of the vault above him. The occasional lonely howl of a wolf hunting in the forests around him inspired only awe, not fear.

It wasn't until they had crossed the mountains and encamped at Selymbria, on the Sea of Marmora, a day's march from Constantinople, that he saw Emma again.

FOUR

The sea fascinated Theo. Never had he seen such an expanse of water. He had thought the rivers mighty, and had been in awe of their rushing, turbulent currents, but the sea was something quite different. In the cold December light, the far side of the Sea of Marmora disappeared over the horizon, its waters lay flat and dull. They gave an impression of immeasurable depth and secrecy. What lay beneath that opaque surface? Now and then, ships would cross—small wooden sailing ships such as those he had often seen in the great ports along the Rhine. Occasionally, far out at the edge of his vision, larger vessels loomed out of the winter mists, then disappeared.

The morning after they made camp, he rose with the dawn, finally free to seek Emma. Baldwin's camp was down by the shore of the sea, he had learned that much. Before he could leave, however, Hugh appeared outside his tent.

"Count Garnier would have you attend morning mass and break fast with him, young sir," he said.

Theo's heart sank, but a summons from the count could not be ignored. He followed Hugh over to his foster father's tent.

"What ails you this morning?" the count asked as Theo squirmed beside him at his campfire. The priests had finished saying mass; he and the count had returned to Garnier's tent. The first meal of the day was spread out on trestle tables: joints of meat, game birds, slabs of thick bread and overflowing flagons of ale. "You are wiggling around like a dog with fleas, and you haven't eaten a thing. Are you not well?"

"I'm fine, my lord. Fine," Theo answered. He grabbed a rib of venison and chewed at it. Normally he would have wolfed it down, but today the meat was dry in his mouth. He couldn't swallow. In his hurry to finish the meal and seek out Emma, he quaffed an overlarge mouthful of ale and choked on it.

When he was finally released, he had to restrain himself from running. He skirted the main tents and headed for the shore, almost frantic with impatience. The camp was noisy with the usual morning bustle. Children ran screaming underfoot, mothers called, men swore. A donkey brayed and was answered by another far in the distance. The smoke from innumerable fires mingled to cast a pall over the whole vast encampment. The smells of roasting meat, animal dung and unwashed bodies were so thick, they were almost visible. Theo kicked through the refuse that was already beginning to pile up, and hurried even more.

He came up to a tent, and heard a whining, bickering argument break out on the other side of it. A few sharp words stilled it; Theo's heart jumped as he recognized Emma's voice. He moved cautiously around the tent. Lord Baldwin's three children were sitting around the fire, finishing up their morning meal; Emma was with them.

Godvere's voice called from another, larger tent nearby.

"Emma, bring them to me now. I wish them to stay with me for a while. You may see to the washing."

Emma rose, looked up and saw Theo. She started, then put a finger to her lips and gestured toward the children.

Wait, she mouthed silently.

Theo backed into the bushes. A few minutes later, he heard a rustle, and Emma emerged, looking slightly disheveled and flushed.

"How good it is to see you!" she exclaimed. "I've been thinking of you all these miles since Hungary." The words burst out, and then she clapped a hand to her mouth. "I mean—" she added hastily, drawing herself up and making a quick attempt to recover her dignity. "I wondered how you were."

"I would have sought you out sooner," Theo answered, "but I could not." He, too, made an effort to keep his words light, his manner dignified. He would have liked to appear aloof, but that was impossible. There was no way under heaven he could suppress the smile that spread almost from ear to ear. She had been thinking about him!

"I have the most enormous load of washing to do. Down by the lake . . ."

"I'll go with you," Theo said.

"Not very fitting for a knight," Emma replied, "to keep company with a nursemaid and her laundry!" She had herself back under control and the teasing note had returned to her voice. This time, Theo didn't mind at all.

"I can help you carry it," he began.

"Now, that would be a sight, wouldn't it? A knight *carrying laundry*. No, that would never do. I know a spot where no one will see us. We'll meet there." She pointed to the woods behind Theo. "Go by that path, the one that leads off through the trees. Wait for me at the bottom, by the water's edge. I'll follow as soon as I can."

Theo followed her directions and found himself on a rocky shore nestled into a small, deserted cove. He looked out over the water—sparkling and deep blue today, with small flecks of waves roughening up the surface—and breathed deeply of the tingling air. He felt light and buoyant and unbelievably happy.

Emma appeared almost immediately, her arms full of linens. She dumped them all into the water, wet them, rubbed them with handfuls of greasy soap, then set to rinsing them and beating them on the rocks. All the while, she kept up a stream of chatter, as if she were feeling self-conscious, afraid perhaps of having seemed too bold. Theo let the words flow over him, only half listening. He was much more concerned with just watching her. Suddenly, she stopped the idle talk and sat back. Her face became serious.

"I think there may be trouble coming, Theo," she said. "It might be well for you to be prepared."

"How so?" Theo asked. It was amazing how the wind coming in off the sea tangled her hair into a forest of black curls, he thought.

"I heard my lord Baldwin talking to the duke last night at supper. It seems that Hugh of Vermandois has already arrived at Constantinople. They say he received wondrous gifts from the emperor Alexius himself, and indeed the reports are so lush that my lord is thinking of going on ahead to get his own share before the rest of you pile in. But there are other rumors as well, and they're more troubling."

"Other rumors?" Theo asked. "Of what sort?" His mind was not really on what she was saying. On a splendid day such as this, he did not want to hear rumors of trouble. It was still hard to believe that Emma was actually here. It was hard to believe how happy her presence made him, too, and that was giving him pause for thought.

"Well, some say that, gifts or no gifts, Hugh and all his men are being held prisoner."

"Do Baldwin and the duke give any substance to that talk?" Reluctantly, Theo began to pay attention to what Emma was saying, but he knew very well how easily rumors spread around the camp, and knew also that most of them were sheer inventions.

Emma paused and pushed a wet strand of hair out of her eyes. Washing the clothes had brought the color to her cheeks, and Theo thought she looked exceedingly fair.

"They do," she said.

"It's probably just nonsense."

"Probably. But I know the duke and Lord Baldwin are worried that when the men hear the rumors they will be angry. The common soldiers and the archers and others are expecting a great deal when we reach Constantinople, you know. They have been told they can rest there until all the great lords and princes have assembled with their armies, and they will be given all they need for their comfort. The way has been hard so far, Theo—they feel they deserve a reward, not punishment. At least, that is what the good duke says. My lord Baldwin cares not a whit about his men's feelings or comfort. He worries only about his own interests."

"Nonsense, surely," Theo said. "The men are much too afraid of the duke to disobey him. We are not the rabble that Peter the Hermit's army was," he added, echoing Amalric's words. Surely Emma exaggerated. After all, women loved to gossip. This army would remain disciplined, Theo was certain of it.

"Still," Emma said, "perhaps you should keep alert." She bent back to her laundry and picked up a garment. As she beat it against a rock, Theo saw that her fingers were red and swollen. The December wind off the Sea of Marmora that was tousling her hair so delightfully was cold, and the water, he realized, must be frigid.

"You must let me help," he said, and bent to pick up another piece of clothing. He flung it against the rock with vigor, but most of it slapped into the water. Spray dashed up and drenched Emma.

"My thanks, Theo! You are indeed of great assistance!"

Theo crimsoned. "I'm sorry," he began. What a fool he must look! Then he sputtered as a spray of water, aimed expertly by Emma, hit him.

Emma let out a peal of laughter and fell back against the bank.

"Your face! If only you could see your face! You

look like a rabbit that's just seen the biggest hound of its life!"

Theo leaped back to his feet, humiliated.

"Oh, Theo, I'm sorry. I'm not laughing at you. It's just . . . It's just, your face was so funny!" Her mouth twitched and she burst into another gale of laughter.

A wave of anger surged through Theo. He scowled. He was not used to being laughed at by a maid.

Emma sobered immediately. "Please," she said. "Stay with me. Do not go away angry because I am such a nitwit. I will not laugh anymore, I promise!" She fastened her eyes upon him, pleading, all trace of mockery gone.

The anger and humiliation melted away. Theo heaved a huge sigh. There was no way he could refuse that look.

By the time he returned to his own camp, he had forgotten all about her warning. It came back to him with a jolt, however, as soon as he arrived.

†　　　†　　　†

"The count wishes to see you immediately," William said. The groom's face was tense, his brow furrowed.

"What is it?" Theo asked.

"I know not, sir," William answered.

Theo knew at once the man was lying. He debated for a moment whether to press him further, then decided against it. The count would tell him soon enough if anything was afoot. He shrugged, and made for Garnier's tent.

The sound of loud, furious voices carried over to the edge of the clearing. Theo could make out the count's voice and, to his surprise, Godfrey's as well. Something must have happened indeed if the duke was that angry. He pushed through the tent flap warily. Once inside, he stood waiting to be noticed.

"There is no excuse," the duke stormed. "How many men are missing?"

"At least five knights and squires, with all their foot soldiers and archers. They must have slipped away before dawn." The count's voice was low and trembled with tightly controlled anger. He passed a hand over his brow and turned his eyes away from Godfrey's, catching sight of Theo as he did so.

"Ah, Theo." He gave a sigh of relief. "You are well come, my son. I have need of you here." He turned toward a group of men standing behind him. Theo recognized them as the most loyal of the count's knights—friends all, and known to him since boyhood. "You will ride with Aimery and these others. Some of our knights have gone berserk and have ridden off with all their men. We discovered their absence just after you left this morning. Already tales have reached us that they have attacked a village nearby and pillaged it. This insanity must be stopped. Alexius will not tolerate it. He will send his forces—" Garnier's control over his words slipped and his voice broke. Theo could imagine only too well what the count was thinking. This army was not to follow in the footsteps of Peter the Hermit's band. They were to be a true crusader army, fighting only for God and for the liberation of Jerusalem.

"You must go after them and stop them." He turned back to the other knights and addressed their leader, Aimery. "Take as many of the men as you need and leave now. At once!"

Theo bowed to his foster father, and bowed again to the duke. He backed out of the tent.

So, Emma had been right, he thought as he ran for his campsite. He must not take her words so lightly in future.

"William!" he called as he reached his tent. "Saddle Centurion. Make him ready for battle." He pushed into the tent and began to dress himself in his metal-ringed leather tunic. Of course, it wouldn't really be a battle, he told himself. They wouldn't be fighting their own men. Still . . .

His blood pounded in his ears as he raced back out. William held Centurion ready. Theo's hands, as he took the reins, shook slightly. He grasped the pommel of his saddle to steady them. He must not look like an excitable, untried boy in front of his groom. When he had got himself under control, he turned back to William.

"You knew, didn't you," he said. "You knew they were going to leave the camp."

"One of the grooms . . ."

"Why didn't you say something, or warn me?" Even as he asked the question, Theo knew it was useless. There was a brotherhood among the grooms that excluded even the most beloved masters, and he was certainly not one of those. "Never mind," he said. He put his foot in the stirrup and swung himself up into the saddle. "Is there food enough in my saddlebags?"

"Yes, master. For several days at least. And two skins each of water and wine." The groom looked relieved.

Theo hesitated. I should discipline him, he thought. He should have told me what he had learned. If I can't count on his loyalty . . . But there was nothing he could do at the moment. When I return, he told himself. William cannot go unpunished. He frowned. This business of being a master was difficult.

A shout called him to attention.

"Theo! Are you ready?" It was Amalric. "Godfrey has given me permission to ride with you. What fun! At last we will see some excitement!" He galloped heavily over to Theo, then reined in his charger with a yank that caused the animal to shake its head angrily and foam at the bit.

"You do your beast damage," Theo said. Amalric's exuberance grated on him. Did he not realize the enormity of the situation? The whole crusade was in danger.

Amalric reached over to throw an arm around Theo's shoulders. His eyes were bright, his cheeks flushed. His enthusiasm was contagious, and in spite of himself, Theo felt his own heart begin to race.

† † †

It was not until morning of the next day that they reached the village the crusaders had raided. They saw smoke rising from the site long before the houses themselves could be seen. Theo and Amalric rode side by side, as usual. Amalric kept up a constant stream of talk as they drew near, but Theo gradually fell silent. He looked around him with growing dread. No birds sang in the trees. He listened in vain for barking dogs. They rounded a bend in the path and the village itself came into view. Nearly every house was burned to the ground; some were still smoldering. There was no sign of life anywhere. A few sacks of grain lay spilt in the middle of the road. The body of a cat lay beside them under a seething blanket of flies. Theo felt his gorge rise. He and Amalric reined in their horses and stared. Finally, Amalric spoke.

"The townsfolk have taken to the hills, I warrant," he said. "Those who were left . . ." The words came out halting and uncertain, unlike his usual breezy manner. He shrugged his shoulders and tried to force the enthusiasm back into his voice. "We'll catch up with the scoundrels who did this, never fear, and take them back to face the duke. That will teach them a lesson!"

"Our own men." Theo's voice was heavy with disbelief. "Our own men destroyed this village, Amalric, and it was a Christian village."

"We'll catch them. They'll be punished." Amalric's face was blank. He didn't meet Theo's eyes. "These things happen in war. It can't be helped."

"We're not at war here." Theo stopped as Amalric dug spurs into his horse with a vicious kick and forged away. He stared after his friend. Amalric might be able to find excuses, to make some sense out of this, but he, Theo, could not.

It took eight days to find the renegade knights and soldiers—eight days of following behind and traveling through ruined villages and ravaged countryside. It seemed the soldiers had, indeed, gone mad. Here and there, Theo caught sight of survivors, but any who saw them ran quickly for the shelter of the woods.

"Should we not stay and help them?" he asked. It seemed to him that they must do *something* to atone for the terrible harm their own men had done. But Aimery just shook his head.

"We can help them best by leaving them alone. They want no more of us." His face was grim, etched with lines Theo had not noticed before.

By the time they did catch up to the marauding army, the renegades had had their fill of violence and looting, and were on their way back. Count Garnier's men took them under immediate arrest, but they seemed little chastened. Their saddlebags bulged, and they were red-eyed from carousing. Theo was sickened by the sight of them. Not so Amalric, however, who seemed to have recovered all of his original excitement. He pointed to a soldier who wore a stained rag tied around his head.

"Look, Theo, blood! That one has seen battle!"

"Battle? Cutting down unarmed villagers? Do you call that battle?" Theo's words were heavy with disgust. For the moment, Amalric sickened him as much as the soldiers did. This time, it was Theo who turned and rode away.

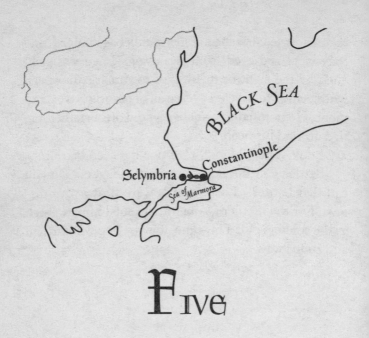

Five

By Yuletide, they were encamped on the stony, sparsely grassed hills outside the walls of Constantinople. The weather was raw and cold, although as yet there was no snow. The priests celebrated the Christmas masses with the domes and spires of all the churches of the great city looming behind them. Theo had never seen such a city before; he was in a frenzy of excitement to explore it. The emperor Alexius was cautious, however. It wasn't until the Christmas celebrations were over that he began to allow small groups in. Amalric was quick to invite Theo to investigate the pleasures of the town's taverns with him, but Theo demurred. His friendship with Amalric was back on its sound footing, and he had managed to convince himself that his judgment of his friend was too harsh, but there was so much else he wanted to see in the city. Then Emma appeared at his campsite early one morning before he had even eaten.

"Theo!" She stood before him, breathless, and a little uncertain. "I have the day to myself and permission to visit the city. Will you go with me?"

He didn't hesitate. Emma would be the ideal person to explore Constantinople with. Besides, he had had little opportunity to seek her out in the past few days, and he had missed her.

"Most certainly, I will," he answered. "I have no duties today—I will ask permission of the count."

Within the hour, they presented themselves at the massive, metal-studded gate at the western edge of the city. Emma pressed through it eagerly and pulled Theo with her. Before them, tree-lined streets and alleys beckoned. Enormous houses of stone, unlike any Theo had seen before, sat surrounded by gardens, beautiful even in the cold of winter.

"I thought the churches of Cologne magnificent," he murmured in awe, "but these surpass even them."

"Truly," Emma agreed. "I could never have imagined such places. They are not covered in gold, though, as was said."

"And the streets are not laden with jewels," Theo added with a laugh.

"But they are wonderful, are they not?"

"They are," Theo said. There was something about the grace and the symmetry of the city that pleased him to the depths of his soul. A man could be happy living in such a place, he thought. The glory and the thrill of war seemed remote and unreal in such a setting.

The marketplace, where they had been told they could find all manner of foods and merchandise, was their main destination, but they lost themselves repeatedly in the maze of streets. Only after stumbling upon the old Roman aqueduct did they find it. The immense stone columns of the waterway towered over them, dwarfing all the buildings around. These pillars supported the gigantic open stone pipeline, built so efficiently by the Romans, that still brought the city's supply of water coursing down from the hills. Theo and Emma stood for a moment, heads tilted back, gawking at the spillway far above them; then they moved on into the market.

As soon as they entered, Theo was overwhelmed with the sights, sounds and smells of it. As he sniffed in the smoky, spice-scented air, the smells wafted around him. Some he could identify—vanilla, cloves, herbs of many kinds—and others were strange to him. Color and confusion reigned. The owners of the stalls called out ceaselessly, hawking their wares, until their voices blended into one loud jumble. The sound of thousands of tiny tapping hammers led him, with Emma in tow, to an area where men battered out platters of silver and copper. Looms thumped and clattered as women wove brightly hued wool into shawls and blankets.

"Oh, look, Theo—shoes! My lady gave me a few coppers and I mean to have a pair." Emma darted over to a stall and began to sort through the assembled footwear. The stall owner, a large, florid, black-haired woman with snapping dark eyes, unleashed a torrent of words at her.

"Greek, I expect," Emma said in an aside to Theo. "I know not a word of it." Undaunted, she held up the pair of soft leather shoes she had chosen and began to bargain with wild, expressive sweeps of her hands. The woman answered with gestures of her own, and an even greater flood of language. To Theo's astonishment, they seemed to understand each other completely. A deal was struck and Emma handed over her few coppers. Then there was nothing for it but to put her new shoes on immediately. She plomped herself down on the cobblestones beside the stall, ripped off her old worn shoes and bound the new ones on. She leaped to her feet and took Theo's arm.

"Are they not fine?" she asked at least ten times as they moved on, stopping each time to stick out a foot and admire it.

Next, they made their way to the food stalls. The aromas were irresistible, the foodstuffs exotic and enticing. They bought sizzling hot, fragrantly spiced meat pies that tasted strongly of mutton and garlic, and washed them down with a light, warm, pleasant-tasting mead. They tried the small black fruit called olives. When Emma made a face at the sour, flat taste, Theo mocked her, then persevered until he began to like them. They tried a strong goat cheese wrapped in grape leaves and drizzled with oil from the olives. Finally, they pushed on through the throngs of people to the other side of the market, and found themselves on a wide, spacious avenue adorned with statues and columns, and dotted with tree-filled plazas that gave shelter from the nipping wind.

"Look!" Theo exclaimed suddenly. "The Hippodrome!" He had heard so much of this stadium—famous for the public games and spectacles that had taken place there ever since the time of the Romans.

"Let's peek in," Emma said. "There's a gate. It's closed, but we can see through." She ran over to it. Theo caught up to her and peered through the iron railings. He could see a vast oval enclosure, ringed with stone tiers. He had heard that over a hundred thousand people could be seated in the Hippodrome. Several tall columns ran in a straight line lengthwise down the center of it. Today, it stood vast and empty, but in Theo's mind it was crowded with spectators. Their roar filled his head. Chariots pulled by crazed, frantic horses careened around the track.

One obelisk was sheathed in gleaming bronze; another column was topped with three serpents' heads holding aloft a tripod that shone golden in the weak winter sun. This was a pagan monument, Theo knew, dedicated to the old Roman god Apollo. The western Christian church disapproved of such things as these and the many other heathen icons that the Byzantine Christians kept by them, but the beauty of the monument entranced him nonetheless.

Emma was eager to go on. Beyond the Hippodrome was Saint Sophia, the Hagia Sophia—one of the oldest and most revered churches in Christendom. Theo could see its dome towering over all the other buildings, even over the Great Palace of the emperor Alexius himself.

"There, Emma. That is where I want to go." Of all the holy churches, the Hagia Sophia was the one Theo most wanted to see. There, he could kneel and pray.

I will pray for the success of our crusade, he thought. Here, it can really begin. The memory of the destroyed Christian villages flickered through his mind, but he pushed it firmly aside. That is not how it will be, he resolved. From here, we go on renewed. From here, the crusade will be a glory to God, and nothing else.

They entered the courtyard, then directed their steps to the small door at the side. Only the emperor himself, Theo had been told, could use the main entrance. Once inside the church, they passed through a low, arched doorway surmounted by a glowing mosaic of the Virgin Mary holding the child Jesus on her lap, with the great emperors Justinian and Constantine paying homage on either side of her. Theo stopped so suddenly that Emma bumped into him, and he heard her gasp, echoing his own sudden intake of breath. Never could he have imagined what now lay before him. Above, the shining dome stretched up higher than the tower of any church Theo had ever seen. The circular vastness was so great that Theo felt almost dizzy with the sense of space. All the columns and arches were intricately carved; the walls and ceiling glowed with the rich colors of the mosaics and paintings that covered every surface. The figures of Jesus and his disciples looked down on them from paintings illuminated with gold. Countless windows let in streams of light. Around the top ran a gallery enriched with a filigree of ironwork and colonnaded with smaller arches that duplicated the taller arches below. A magnificent cross blazed out from behind the altar, dominating all with a golden splendor of its own.

Theo brought his gaze back to look at the people around him. The church was crowded, filled with ordinary people as well as with men and women who were obviously of the nobility, but of a nobility very different from what Theo knew. On the whole, the knights of the German and Frankish lands were a rough lot. Their ladies dressed colorfully but modestly in woollens during the winter months, and in linen shifts when the weather was warm. The knights themselves worried little about their attire other than to ensure it was warm enough in the cold weather. The clothing of these nobles, however, dazzled Theo's eyes. The ladies' dresses shimmered and whispered with the softness of silk. Their hair was ornately styled and dripping with jewels. More jewels sparkled on their necks, arms and fingers. Shawls of gossamer wool were draped over their shoulders. If anything, the men outshone the women: they, too, were brilliantly dressed and flashing with gems. They knelt to pray on tiny, many hued carpets.

Suddenly, Theo was uncomfortably aware of his dirty, travel-stained tunic and the coarseness of his drab, heavy cloak. He slid one leg in front of the other to cover a rip in his hose, but no one was paying the slightest attention to him. He tore his eyes away from the lords and ladies and dropped to his knees, fixing his eyes on the cross. Emma sank down beside him.

They remained praying for a long time. At last, Theo stood. When he glanced down at Emma, she was still staring at the altar; there were tears on her cheeks. She looked suddenly small and vulnerable, and he felt a wave of protectiveness surge through him as he reached down to help her to her feet.

"It is God's work we do, is it not?" Her words came out in the barest, but fiercest, of whispers.

"Of course it is. It has to be." Theo turned his back

on the brilliant personages, who seemed to be gossiping with each other as much as praying, and put them out of his mind. It was the crusade that mattered. Nothing else.

On the way out, Theo spied an old woman in the courtyard. She sat hunched under a woollen shawl, warmed only by a small fire. In front of her, spread out on a carpet, were bunches of sweetly scented dried herbs and roses. On an impulse, he stopped. He bent over her offerings and chose one. Gravely, he turned to Emma and gave it to her.

Emma took it with a startled, sideways glance at him. Then she lowered her eyes and buried her nose in the bouquet. "No one has ever . . ." The words came out muffled. "Thank you." It was so quiet, he barely heard.

"You should have come with us!" Amalric exclaimed the next morning. "We found a lively tavern, with men who made music and wenches who danced to it. The wine they make here is so strong my head is still spinning! You would have had a far better time with me than you had traipsing around churches with a servant maid!"

Theo smiled, but didn't answer. He thought not.

† † †

At first, Theo welcomed the pause at Constantinople, but as the weeks passed, he became restless again.

Some remnants of Peter the Hermit's forces arrived in the camp. Theo was present when Duke Godfrey interviewed them.

"Treason," they maintained. "Nothing less than treachery on the part of the imperial forces of Alexius led to our defeat."

"The duke does not believe them," Amalric said, "and nor do I. They just seek excuses for their own failure."

Theo was inclined to agree, but he heard the soldiers around him grumbling. They, too, were becoming impatient with the delay.

"If we could only go on!" Amalric was indignant. "Alexius has no right to hold us up here."

"But we must wait for the other lords who are coming to meet us," Theo answered.

"We could wait on the other side of Constantinople. He could let us pass. The only reason he keeps us cooling our heels here is because Godfrey will not swear allegiance to him."

Theo knew Amalric was right.

"My lord has only one master, Henry, the emperor of the Holy Roman Empire. He cannot swear loyalty to another," Amalric growled.

Again, Theo agreed.

Time dragged. Theo took to walking the camp from end to end, usually finishing up at the city walls. They towered above him, blank and forbidding.

It snowed, lightly at first, then more heavily. Theo found it hard to keep himself warm at night in his small tent. He slept wrapped in his woollen cloak and covered with a bearskin, but still woke stiff and cold in the frosty early mornings. Centurion, on the other hand, delighted in the winter weather. His coat grew rough and thick, and he downed the rations of four normal horses.

"Hugh of Vermandois has sworn the oath," Amalric reported with a sneer as he sought Theo out one morning. "Alexius's lapdog, that's all he is. The emperor thought Hugh would persuade the duke to give in and sign as well, but my lord Godfrey sent him back with a flea in his ear, I tell you."

Perhaps not a wise move, Theo thought. He was proven right when the supplies coming from the emperor suddenly ceased.

Angered by the short rations, the men erupted. Led by Godfrey's brother Baldwin, they began to raid the suburbs of Constantinople. Alexius reacted quickly.

"We are to move to Pera," Count Garnier told Theo as they ate together one morning. "The emperor has been most tactful. Pera is only a short distance away, and he suggests that we will be more sheltered from the winter winds there, but I think his real reason is that his imperial police will be able to watch and control us more closely there. I must say I cannot blame him. If Lord Godfrey cannot keep even his own brother in check . . ."

Theo looked at his foster father in surprise. It was the closest he had ever heard the count come to criticizing the duke. Garnier must be troubled, indeed.

Amalric, of course, was mightily offended. "They think us nothing but barbarians," he raged. "They treat us like thieves!"

"With good reason," Theo replied, but the behavior of the Byzantines had angered him as well. He had accompanied Count Garnier to a feast given by some of the nobles in the city, and although the visitors had dressed in their finest, Theo had been painfully aware of the disparaging glances cast their way. More than one elegant eyebrow had been raised at the rude manners of the Frankish knights. The Franks, on their part, spent the next few days mocking the effete manners of the Byzantines, but underlying their jokes was a bitter resentment.

More time passed. Still the other lords did not appear; still the emperor and Godfrey quarreled. Life in the camp around Pera settled into a routine that soon turned to boredom. Godfrey and his men were lodged within the city, but their families and all the others, including Count Garnier and his men, were encamped just outside.

Theo had fallen into the habit of meeting with Emma in the evenings to talk. He knew a few tongues wagged at this, but life in the camp was informal, and he cared little about the opinions of others. The count saw no harm in their friendship, and that was what mattered most to him. Emma always had the latest camp gossip, and she had a way of exaggerating the most trifling of stories until they became so ridiculous that the two of them usually ended up in gales of laughter. It was a relief to Theo to spend time with her after the tension of daily life in the camp. Amalric grew so frenzied with hatred against the Byzantine emperor that he could speak or think of nothing else. He was not alone in his feelings—indeed, most of the camp felt the way he did—but Theo could take only so much of his ranting.

Amalric had also angered Theo by teasing him about Emma, and had made a coarse, insinuating jest. Theo had reacted with an explosion of anger, and they would have come to blows if Amalric had not backed down. After his anger had cooled, however, Theo was shocked at his reaction. He had not thought that he could get so irate over such a thing. Just what did this girl mean to him? She seemed to be on his mind constantly. Somehow, Emma was different from the other girls he had dallied with, and he dared not behave with her as he had with the others. Friendly as she was, she held herself aloof from everyone. He had once seen another young knight throw an arm carelessly around her, only to find himself flat on his back in the mud. Emma was definitely not to be trifled with.

The end of March arrived. Winter was over and the weather began to grow warm; Holy Week was fast approaching. News spread that the other crusading armies were near. The tension in the camp reached an unbearable peak. Surely now, Theo thought, Alexius would let them move on. Instead, feeling perhaps that the other leaders would support him in his demand for oaths of allegiance, Alexius began to restrict the crusaders' supplies further. First, he withheld fodder for the horses; then, as Holy Week drew nearer, he cut off supplies of fish and bread. This was the final insult. How could they not have fish during Holy Week?

The crusaders exploded. Several of the knights led their men in raids on neighboring villages. Count Garnier kept his own knights and troops in order, but even the most loyal of them, Theo included, began to chafe at the bit.

"Things cannot go on like this," he told Emma one evening.

"No, they cannot," she agreed. "I fear for what is going to happen. It cannot be good."

Theo fell silent beside her.

On the Wednesday evening of Holy Week itself, Godfrey called a conference in his tent.

"Come with me," the count said to Theo. "I like not the sound of this."

They arrived to find the other nobles already assembled, Baldwin foremost among them. Godfrey was speaking. Theo had never seen him so inflamed.

"The emperor persists in his impossible demands. He has denied us passage across the Bosphorus, and he insists on my oath. That I will not give. The time has come for force. We attack Constantinople tomorrow."

Theo could not believe what he was hearing. Attack Constantinople? Constantinople was one of Christendom's most holy cities, second only to Jerusalem! Attack the emperor Alexius himself?

†   †   †

The next morning as he prepared for battle in the darkness before dawn, Theo moved as if he were weighted down with chains of iron. Again they were to wage war against Christians! The Byzantines were hateful, but they were the crusaders' own people. *They* were not the enemy he had sworn to conquer!

Centurion's breath steamed into the cool air. In the darkness around him, Theo could hear the clink of metal, the squeak of leather being adjusted, tightened. The occasional oath broke the stillness, but there was an unusual quiet. No one, it seemed, was going into this attack with bravado. Theo did not speak to William. He had disciplined his groom for not reporting what he had known about the planned outbreak of the count's and Godfrey's men, and William had been sullen and resentful ever since.

When all was ready, Theo accepted William's hand up and swung into the saddle. He reined Centurion in and guided him toward the gathering of Count Garnier's knights and squires. The count greeted him soberly as Theo fell in between his foster father and

Aimery. In silence, they walked their horses to the edge of Pera to wait for Duke Godfrey.

As they drew near to Pera's walls, pandemonium erupted. Cries broke out from within. Flames shot into the air. Men shouted; women screamed. The town gates were flung open, and Godfrey galloped out, closely followed by his knights and their squires. They had taken their revenge: the houses they had been lodged in were burning to the ground.

In an instant, all was mad confusion. Trumpets blared, war cries echoed across the hillside. When Count Garnier gave the signal, his trumpeters added to the cacophony, and he charged to join the duke. Belatedly, Theo urged Centurion to follow, and the warhorse burst into a gallop. All around Theo, men and horses jostled and jockeyed for position. The thunder of hooves and the cries of the knights filled the air. Dust rose in choking waves. The men in the crusading army fell in behind their leaders and galloped toward Constantinople.

Theo found himself riding so close to the count that their knees brushed. The crush of other animals and riders beside and around him blotted out all else. Blindly, he gave Centurion his head and concentrated on keeping up with his foster father. His heart was beating so loudly that his ears rang with the force of it, and he thought it would tear through the very walls of his chest. There was no time now to think about what they were doing, no time to think about who they were about to attack. He gasped for breath in the thick, suffocating air.

The army strung out as it thundered across the bridge at the headwaters of the Golden Horn, then reassembled outside the walls of Constantinople itself. For a moment, there was a pause. Theo struggled to calm himself. In front of him the great city slept, seemingly unprepared for attack.

Trumpets split the early morning. Godfrey shouted an order. Chaos erupted around Theo again. Yelling their battle cries, the duke's men charged the gate that led to the palace. Theo glimpsed Amalric among the foremost. Then, suddenly, as his own group rallied to follow Godfrey, Theo saw archers appear on the walls. Again, he spurred Centurion on and charged forward beside Count Garnier, but this time he held his breath. They were driving straight into the archers. He shrank in his saddle, and his stomach tightened into a ball as he braced himself against the onslaught of arrows that was sure to come. Incredibly, the first volley passed harmlessly over their heads.

When the gate did not give way under the foot soldiers' assault, Godfrey's men drew back in confusion. At that moment, all the other gates opened and Alexius's troops poured out. Again, Theo braced himself, but again, incredibly, the troops did not attack. They halted outside the walls, facing the now flustered duke and his army. Foot soldiers with halberds glinting in the first pale rays of the sun arrayed themselves deliberately in front of their mounted knights. The archers high on the top of the wall above them let loose another volley of arrows. Once more, the missiles flew over the crusaders' heads.

Godfrey's army froze, every man in his place, waiting for the duke's signal. For what seemed like an eternity, Theo watched as the two opposing forces faced each other. Then, instead of crying out the expected command to attack, Godfrey wheeled his mount around and galloped off the field. After an instant of silent disbelief, his men turned their horses and followed him. Aghast, Theo looked at the count. The count returned his stare with his mouth set in a hard, grim line.

As they retreated, Theo looked back over his shoulder. The domes and spires of Constantinople gleamed in the sunlight, unconquered, inviolable. He could make no sense of his feelings. Relief because they had not fought fellow Christians, and because he was alive. But his heart still thudded and his ears still rang. Gradually, the terror of the charge drained away, but in its place rose a vast emptiness.

He felt—cheated.

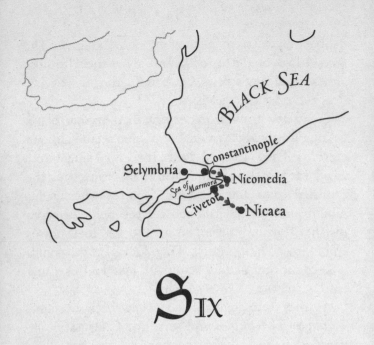

S_{IX}

In the aftermath of this debacle, Godfrey finally consented to take the oath of allegiance to Alexius. The ceremony was held on Easter Sunday. Godfrey, Baldwin and their leading lords swore to acknowledge the emperor as overlord of the campaign, and to hand over to the Byzantine officials any reconquered land that had previously belonged to the emperor. Theo saw Baldwin's mouth twist at that pledge, and remembered Emma telling him of Baldwin's greed. No land would be relinquished by the duke's brother if he could help it, oath or no oath, Theo thought.

Following the ceremony, the emperor organized a mammoth celebration. Even though Alexius had been horrified by Godfrey's attack during Holy Week itself, he showered gifts and money upon the assembled knights, and ended the festivities with a banquet of huge proportions. Then Godfrey and all his troops were transported across the Bosphorus, the narrow stretch of water that separated Constantinople from the lands to the east. They marched on to an encampment at Pelecanum, on the road to Nicomedia. There they would wait for the other crusading armies to catch up with them.

The weather melted into spring. One fine morning, Amalric and Theo stood together on a rise that danced with scarlet poppies and white and yellow daisies. The long grasses whispered around their legs. In the distance, toward Constantinople, a cloud of dust arose.

"That will be Bohemond of Taranto," Amalric announced with satisfaction. "Finally. They say he did not hesitate to give his oath to Alexius, but demanded to be named commander-in-chief of all the imperial forces in Asia."

"And did he get his wish?"

Amalric made a face. "Alexius waffled, what else? Gave him some vague assurances. Bohemond's brother, Tancred, was more clever. He slipped by

Constantinople at night and avoided Alexius altogether. But wait until Raymond arrives. Then we'll see
the fur fly."

"Why?" Theo asked. These political wranglings
irked him more and more. The crusaders were all
sworn to the same cause; why did there need to be so
much dissention?

"Raymond is the count of Toulouse. Connected to
the royal houses of Spain, and very full of himself, he
is. Lord Godfrey says Raymond is immensely jealous
of Bohemond and feels he should be the leader."

Theo shrugged his shoulders irritably.

The powerful Bishop Adhemar of Le Puy was next
to arrive with all his forces. Theo had heard many stories about this man. A holy cleric he was, but also a
formidable soldier. Theo watched with interest as the
bishop rode into the encampment. He sat tall in his
saddle at the forefront of his army, helmetless, his iron
gray hair flowing to his shoulders. An impressive man,
even from this distance. He radiated strength and
assurance.

Raymond sent word that he would join the crusading armies later, as did Robert, duke of Normandy,
the final lord for whom they waited.

"Now," Amalric exulted, "now we can go!"

They left by the end of April on a bright and golden
day. Loaded down with supplies and equipment, they
put all resentments behind them. Nearly a hundred
thousand strong now, scarlet crosses of Christ vivid on

their chests and shoulders, the crusaders felt their spirits rise, and the mood throughout the ranks was again one of optimism and wild excitement. The heavy, bone-shaking gait of the warhorses was too uncomfortable to bear for long periods of time, so Theo and the other knights rode lighter palfreys. Their grooms and squires, mounted on nags or mules, led the more formidable, heavier animals. Behind them was a special detachment of engineers provided by the emperor Alexius.

Pennants flew in the brisk spring breezes. There was a smell of fresh earth and a newness to the air. The jangling, clanging sounds of an immense army on the march and all its followers echoed back from the hills on the one side, and over the shining blue of the long arm of the Sea of Marmora on the other.

It was an incredible, impossible, unbelievably unwieldy procession. The last of the pilgrims did not even set out until far into the day—long after the glittering head of the army had passed out of sight and was well on its way. Theo often turned in his saddle to look back at the people behind him. The line stretched out as far as he could see.

He could not bring himself to be as jubilant as the others. Eight months, he thought. We have been on the road for eight long months. He knew that many in the crusade had assumed they would have been in Jerusalem by now, that the Holy City would have been long conquered. Instead . . . Memories of the hardships they had already endured crowded into his head. The atrocities . . .

Eight months. And they had only just begun.

† † †

They camped that night at Nicomedia, on the way to their first objective, Nicaea, a Turkish city on the shores of the Ascanian Lake. There the battle to liberate the Holy Lands would truly begin.

Theo was called to a conference in Godfrey's tent almost as soon as he had finished making his camp. Leaving William to see to the fire and boil up a stew for their dinner, he made his way quickly to Count Garnier, and they went on together. Godfrey was speaking as they pushed aside the flap to his tent and entered. He had recovered from the disaster at Constantinople and, now that they were actually on their way, he was back to his old self. Looking at him, Theo told himself for perhaps the hundredth time that the duke had made the wisest decision at Constantinople—indeed, the only decision. It would have been a catastrophe if he had pressed the attack. The crusaders could not have won, and hundreds of Christians would have been killed.

But Theo was still troubled by the feeling he had had when the duke had turned away. He *had* felt cheated. He had been revolted at the thought of fighting fellow Christians, but sometime during that mad charge his emotions had taken over. All thoughts of God and the crusade's noble purpose had fled his mind, and he had been filled with a wild exultation. He had been ready to fight, fellow Christians or not. Worse, he had been ready—even eager—to kill.

He had not seen Amalric for days after the aborted attack. When they finally did speak together, Amalric had been quick to defend the duke's action. It was obvious to Theo that Amalric was bitterly disappointed at not having done battle, and shared none of Theo's misgivings about these feelings. But Amalric would not hear any criticism of the duke. In any case, Theo could not bring himself to speak about that day, and when Amalric realized this he changed the subject with obvious relief.

"We are in luck," Duke Godfrey was saying as Theo followed his foster father into the tent. "The Seljuk sultan, Kilij Arslan, is away fighting on the eastern frontier. It was he who defeated Peter's army so easily, and perhaps because of that victory he does not take us seriously. If he thinks we will be as easy to conquer, he will soon learn his mistake. Foolishly, he has even left his wife and children in Nicaea."

"And all his treasure," Baldwin put in. His eyes gleamed. Theo could have sworn he was restraining himself with difficulty from licking his lips.

A disturbance at the tent's entrance interrupted them. A man pushed his way in, brushing past protesting guards. He was dirty and ragged, with limp, greasy hair hanging down around his shoulders, but in spite of his appearance, he held himself with the bearing of a king. His eyes shone with a peculiar sort of light. Theo stared at him.

"I am Peter. I have come to join you and bring those of my followers who are still with me to you. You will have need of me." His voice rang out within the tent.

Peter the Hermit himself!

Godfrey rose. He gestured to the guards to leave. "You are welcome," he said. "Your knowledge of this area will be invaluable to us." There was a long silence. No one would speak of Peter's defeat, or the reasons for it, but thoughts of it hung heavily in the air.

"Continue. I would hear your plans." Peter spoke regally, as if graciously giving permission to one of his underlings.

A faint flush colored Godfrey's cheeks. He sat down abruptly.

"We will march cautiously to Nicaea," he said. "I will send engineers ahead to widen the track, which I understand is narrow in places, and scouts to warn us of any possible ambush." He looked meaningfully at Peter. It had been a lack of just this kind of planning that had led to the hermit's downfall.

Amalric stood behind Godfrey. When Theo caught his eye, Amalric raised an eyebrow. His easy-going good humor seemed to be restored. He looked as if he were enjoying himself.

✝   ✝   ✝

They waited at Nicomedia for three days until all the troops were assembled and ready. There were fields here where the armies could spread out and camp. Peter and the remains of his army made their own camp somewhat apart from the others. Theo had heard that the monk was a great preacher, but Peter held no congregation here. He spoke little to anyone and seemed to seethe with a bitterness that escaped only through his burning eyes.

The morning chosen for their departure dawned bright and clear; the sun now gave a hint of the heat that was to come in the months ahead. They rounded the eastern end of the Sea of Marmora and headed for Civetot. The poppy-strewn fields at Civetot pushed out in a triangle into the southern shore of the sea. It was here that Peter's followers had camped, and here where the Turkish army had flooded in after ambushing and destroying Peter's army in the narrow defile to the south. The sultan's men had massacred almost everyone: women, children, old men, priests. Theo gazed at the scene and his mind went back to the three wanderers he had seen in the tavern in Semlin. They must have been here, the girl and the child, camped somewhere on this very plain. The boy—he would have been among the soldiers, fighting. Near the shoreline, a tall tree lent some shade to the field, a cairn of stones on the ground under its branches. What had happened here? What was war really like? The waves of the sea lapped at the shore with deceptive peacefulness. The blood-red poppies swayed in the breeze.

They turned south, through the pass where Peter's men had been ambushed. The engineers had done their work well; the way had been widened, but bones still lay strewn around the entrance and among the rocks at the sides. Human bones—with shreds of skin still stretched over them here and there, and remnants of moldering cloth among them. A series of wooden crosses marked the cleared track. A hush fell over the column of knights as their mounts picked their way through.

"Did you see the huts on the hillsides with roofs thatched with sticks and twigs?" Amalric asked that night when he sought Theo out after his evening meal. "I saw goats on top of one of them, prancing around! One was even eating leaves that were still growing from it." His voice was hard and brittle, full of careless laughter, but there was a new look in his eyes.

It could almost have been fear, Theo thought, but dismissed the idea immediately. Amalric afraid? Impossible. He laughed with him. Yes, he had seen the goats. But in his mind, all he could see were the bones.

† † †

A week's steady marching brought them to Nicaea. As they drew near the city, Theo could see massive walls rising straight out of the water on the western side. The same walls ran around the other three sides; there were towers at regular intervals.

"That will be a tough nut to crack," Amalric said as they drew nearer and the walls loomed high before them. "Now at last I wager we will see real fighting." His face was flushed and eager. Any doubts or fears he might have been harboring had obviously been cast out. He fingered the pommel of his sword nervously; the palfrey he rode danced a few skittish steps as if sensing his excitement. Theo felt his own heart quicken.

The excitement was contagious and traveled quickly throughout the army. Godfrey camped outside the northern wall, while Tancred and Bohemond took the eastern side. Raymond arrived and closed the circle to the south. Men set about entrenching themselves with an almost feverish haste.

The Turkish garrison sent messengers to open negotiations with the armies, but when news came that the sultan and his army had turned back and were now hastening to Nicaea from the south, the crusaders were quick to bring all talks to a halt. Preparations for war began.

Theo sharpened his sword and dagger and polished his shield, then did so all over again. He checked Centurion's bridle, saddle and girthstraps himself, to the annoyance of William, who took it as an insult to his competence. He was keyed up to a fever pitch and jumped to his feet, heart suddenly racing, when Amalric appeared at his fireside late one evening. Amalric had been at the nightly conference in Godfrey's tent, and would bring news of when the attack would come. His friend was scowling, however, all traces of excitement gone.

"The sultan will attack from the south," he said, his voice sullen. "Raymond's army and the Bishop of Le Puy will see all the action. We are to remain here, and not fight at all! The walls must be guarded, the duke says, so that there will be no possibility of forces coming out of the city and attacking our rear." He paced back and forth beside the fire, kicking angrily at the smoldering embers.

Theo felt a wrench of disappointment. Was he never to see battle?

"Perhaps the sultan will not return that way," he said. "Perhaps he will trick us."

"He must come back that way." Amalric glared as if Theo were being deliberately stupid, aimed another kick at the fire, then turned and strode away into the darkness.

He was right. Theo awakened with the dawn to the sound of trumpets and wailing horns on the far side of the city. The camp was up in an instant, everyone desperate to know what was happening, the men in a frenzy at not being allowed to leave their posts.

The battle raged all day. Theo could only hear vague echoes. Now and then, scouts brought news.

The crusaders were beating back the Turks . . . The Turks were massacring the crusaders . . . Theo felt he would go mad at the enforced inaction, and he was not alone. The men were enraged at their helplessness. The walls of the city seemed unmanned, almost deserted, but a cautious foray toward them by several crusaders frantic for battle drew a skyful of arrows. The knights were sent to ride up and down among the foot soldiers and archers, to keep them in their ranks and alert. Theo welcomed the opportunity to do something—anything—but Centurion, who knew that a battle was underway, fought the slow pace his master insisted on. The warhorse was soon covered in sweat and foaming at the mouth as he champed at his bit. Theo needed all his strength and skill to hold the charger in.

It wasn't until night fell that the battle was over. Scouts arrived after dark with the news that the sultan's forces had retreated. Immediately, a delirious, almost insane joy swept away the paralyzing frustration of the previous hours. Shouts and cheers filled the air, and rose even louder when a detachment of Raymond's knights rode triumphantly into the camp, bearing the heads of their vanquished foes on pikes. The knights paraded their trophies before the gates of the city by torchlight, then hurled them into the enclosure within.

"That will show the Turks who they are up against," Amalric gloated, his eyes shining. Then his voice turned heavy with jealousy. "Next time, we must be the ones who fight! They cannot keep us from them now!"

Theo could not answer. Although he was as disappointed as Amalric at not having been part of the battle, he could not get the image of the bloody, impaled heads out of his mind. The taste of bile rose sour in his mouth and he swallowed it down. What was the matter with him, anyway? Did he, after all, have too weak a stomach for a man?

"We suffered many losses," he said finally, but there was a quiver in his voice. "The count of Ghent was killed, I heard."

Only the night before, Theo had seen the count, a slight, quiet man, sitting alone in front of his tent, pensive in the light from his fire. Emma had told him that the count was a great storyteller. Godvere's children would listen to him, entranced, for hours.

"Losses!" Amalric sneered. "Of course there were losses. There is no battle without them." He looked at Theo, his eyes piercing, almost suspicious. "You speak weakly for a knight, my friend."

Theo bristled. His thoughts of the moment before made his voice suddenly harsh. "Do you question my courage?" he snapped. "I am no more afraid of battle than you."

"Of course not," Amalric replied, taken aback. A conciliatory smile immediately replaced the sneer. "Of course not. And we shall see great battles together, you and I. It is our destiny." He threw his arm around Theo's shoulders. "We are going to be heroes, you and I, Theo. We will fight nobly, for fame and glory."

"What about for God?" Theo asked.

"Of course," Amalric replied quickly. "And for God."

† † †

Robert of Normandy finally arrived with his brother-in-law, Stephen, count of Blois, and his cousin Robert, count of Flanders.

"Stephen did not want to come at all," Emma informed Theo, "but his wife forced him to."

With their arrival, the great crusading armies were now all assembled. They dug in, and the siege of Nicaea began in earnest.

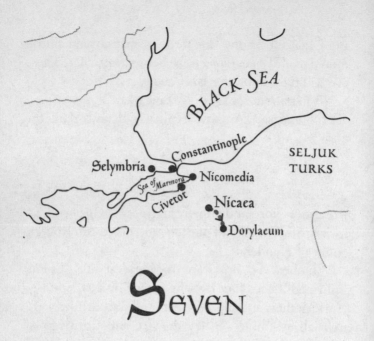

Seven

Theo sat in on the plans for the taking of Nicaea. He soon realized the difficulties facing them.

"The fortifications of the city are formidable," Duke Godfrey told them. "We have sent some of Alexius's engineers in to dig under the walls during the day to undermine them. We've even lit a huge fire under the southern tower. But at night the Turks just repair whatever damage we manage to inflict." He paced back and forth within the narrow confines of his tent. "Worst of all," he continued, "the city is still open to the lake on its western side. They can receive all the supplies they want that way."

"We need boats," Count Garnier said.

"The emperor Alexius has promised to send them. When he does, we can close off the city from the lake," Godfrey replied. "Until then, we can do nothing."

When the boats finally arrived, under the command of the emperor's most trusted engineer, Butumites, Amalric was first with the news to Theo.

"Now," Amalric gloated, "now we can attack, and this time, there will be no denying us. This time, we will fight!"

But when the morning of the planned attack dawned, the crusaders awoke to see the flag of the imperial emperor Alexius flying over the city. The Turks had surrendered to Butumites! His forces had entered the city through the lakeside gates during the night, and the city had been handed over to them.

"It is treachery, pure and simple!" Godfrey exploded, as his knights assembled around him in a hastily called meeting. "Butumites dealt directly with the city; he told us nothing of his dealings. And now he has taken the city for himself!"

Beside him, his brother Baldwin glowered. There was treasure beyond compare in that city—all of it now out of reach of the crusaders.

Tempers were not assuaged by the sight of Turkish

nobles being escorted out of the city to safety by the emperor's troops.

"They've been allowed to buy their freedom—all the nobles and the court officials," Amalric told Theo. "The sultana and her children were escorted to Constantinople and received by the emperor with full honors. All the ransom money has gone to fill *his* coffers. Baldwin is almost inside-out with fury."

Gifts of food arrived from the emperor for every soldier on the crusade. All the leaders received gold and jewels from the sultan's treasury, but these presents were not enough.

"Treason!" The word resounded throughout the camp. "We were the ones who set up the siege. We were the ones who fought the sultan and defeated him. The city should have been ours. The emperor has betrayed us!" Nevertheless, with the capture of Nicaea, word went out that the crusade was a success, and recruits poured into the camps.

They left Nicaea and took the old Byzantine main road across Asia Minor to the Sangarius River, then left the river to climb up a tributary valley to the south. The way was easy and, as they climbed into the hills, the early summer's heat was tempered by a constant breeze. Numerous springs gushed out of the hillsides to quench the thirst of beasts and humans alike. They feared no attack along this stretch, and although scouts were still sent out, discipline relaxed somewhat. Theo rode often with Amalric, but he also managed to find excuses to fall back and ride with Emma as well. Emma caused something of a scandal by choosing to ride horseback, rather than in the wagon with Godvere and her children. Godvere objected furiously, but for some reason Baldwin found the situation amusing and overrode his wife's objections.

"She is, after all, a distant kinswoman of mine," Baldwin announced. "She is entitled to her own will." This was the first time he had ever acknowledged that Emma was more than a servant. When Theo heard this news, he was taken aback.

"Why did you not tell me you were kin to Lord Baldwin?" he demanded as they rode together one day.

"I am very distantly related," Emma replied. "Our family fell on hard times back in the days of my father's father. We have never begged a thing of Lord Baldwin, and he had never seen fit to offer anything— until he sent word that he needed a nursemaid for his children on this crusade."

"But it is not fitting. The whole world thinks you are a servant."

"And a servant I am. I am quite content with it. I'm grateful, in fact, for the opportunity to earn my own way in the world and not be a burden to my poor parents, who have a swarm of other mouths to feed." The words were tart. Emma's face took on an irritated expression that warned Theo off.

"I think, too, my lord may have his own reasons for

humoring me," Emma continued. The irritation vanished and her lips twisted into a wry smile.

"And what would they be?" Theo asked.

"He has been very friendly toward me lately," Emma replied. "More so when we are out of sight of Godvere's wagon. When he rides beside me, his hand will sometimes stray to settle upon my leg."

Theo scowled. "You allow such impertinence?" he asked.

"Impertinence? I am, in fact, his servant, distant relation or not. I owe him a debt. No behavior of his toward me could possibly be considered impertinence."

At this, Theo straightened in his saddle and turned to glare at her. "He has no right."

Emma, however, seemed much less concerned. She laughed. "Don't puff yourself up so, you're worrying your horse. I am well able to take care of myself, thank you, and always have been, but I do it in my own way. It does not serve me to make an enemy of him."

"But still . . ." Theo protested.

"I have perfected a trick of tickling my dear mare with the toe of my shoe in just the right spot to make her shy suddenly," Emma replied calmly. "It invariably takes me out of reach. My lord cannot understand why such a gentle creature is the victim of such nerves. He has even offered to procure me a steadier nag but I, of course, would not dream of allowing him to go to the trouble."

Theo looked at her. He had been thinking of casually reaching for her hand sometime as they rode together, but he reconsidered. He decided it was a risk better not taken.

† † †

The army wound its way slowly through a pass in the hills. The crusaders reached the Blue River and paused there to reassemble. A small Byzantine detachment under one of the emperor's most experienced generals, Taticius, joined them. The detachment, warblooded soldiers all, was welcome, but many muttered that Taticius was no more than the emperor's spy. By the bridge at Leuce, on the Blue River, the leaders decided to divide the army into two sections to facilitate travel, the first to precede the second by a day's interval. The French and the Lorrainers were to be in the second.

Amalric and Theo lounged together by the remains of Theo's morning campfire and watched the vanguard leave with a shared resentment. Although it meant only a day's delay, they chafed at it. It was the first truly hot day of summer and the heat was bothersome. Small insects flew around their heads incessantly, tormenting them.

"If there is any action, they will be the first to see it," Amalric grumbled, swatting at a fly. "They will take all the spoils before we even arrive."

"Spoils!" Theo retorted. "Is that all you think of? You are as bad as Baldwin." The heat and the delay had irritated him so much that he spoke without thinking. He scratched furiously at an itch that was just out of reach below the neck of his leather jerkin. Although the hour was early, sweat was already pouring into his eyes.

"You think yourself such a noble crusader," Amalric shot back, "yet I did not see you refusing your share of the rewards the emperor passed out to us at Nicaea."

Theo jumped to his feet. "A bit of food and a ring! Not so much to accuse me for."

"If there had been more for you, you would have taken it," Amalric said.

"I do not fight for spoils." Theo's anger blazed. "And in this most holy of all wars, all I have heard so far is bickering about what there is to be gained! I want to fight, not loot."

"You rarely have one without the other, and more thanks for that, I say." Amalric rose to his feet as well, and faced Theo. "You'll see. You'll take your fair share when the time comes and bargain for as much more as you can get. You're no different from the rest of us. Except, of course, for your taste in riding companions." He cast a sly glance at Theo, then went on. "For a quick snuggle at night, that I could understand, but to ride with a servant girl during the day, as if she were your equal . . . You make yourself ridiculous there, my friend."

Theo felt the blood rush to his head. There was a quick pressure, a pounding in his ears. His dagger was suddenly in his hand, the point at Amalric's throat.

Amalric took a step backward. His hand went for his own dagger, and then he stopped. His eyes were suddenly as black as stones.

"You would be wise to sheath that, my friend."

Reason returned to Theo like a douse of cold water. He thrust the dagger back into his belt. Pride, however, would not let him apologize.

"You are too free with your opinions, *my* friend," he said.

For a moment, they glared at each other. A voice from the path beyond the campsite startled them both.

"What's this? My two pups snarling at each other? Good, I say. You'll be in fine fettle for the battles to come." A tall figure strode across the clearing toward them. It was Godfrey himself. "And there will be battles, my bloodthirsty young men, trust me. You will have more opportunities than you can count to bloody your swords in the service of Christ. Keep your mettle up, but do not go too far. I will not have fighting within my ranks, remember that." The words were light, but underlaid with iron. In two easy strides, he was across the campsite and heading up the path to his own tent.

He left a silence behind him. Then Amalric spoke.

"I take back my words," he said, his voice carefully controlled. "Your preferences are your own business.

Still . . . ," he threw his arm around Theo's shoulders in his old familiar way and his face relaxed into a smile, "if it's servant girls you like, come with me after we sup tonight. There is a certain wench in the duke's party . . ."

Theo forced himself not to stiffen under Amalric's touch.

Amalric prattled on. "The duke was right," he said. "We need a battle! That is the trouble with us. We are, after all, friends, are we not?"

Theo detached himself. "Yes, of course," he said. If he hesitated, Amalric did not seem to notice it.

It crossed Theo's mind to blurt out that Emma was no mere serving girl, that she was kin, even if distant, to Baldwin, but he kept silent. Emma did not need him to defend her. In fact, he felt certain she would flay him alive for trying it.

† † †

They forged on steadily for the next two days. On the evening of the second, their half of the army had gained on the first contingent, and was within a half day's march from where it was camped, near a town called Dorylaeum. The mood in Godfrey's camp was easier now. The next morning, however, the priests' prayers and the bustle of making ready for departure were interrupted by the arrival of a scout. The horse he was riding was covered in foam and staggering. It foundered even as the man rode up beside Godfrey's tent. He threw the reins to a nearby groom and dashed in, unannounced. Theo and Amalric, waiting nearby, were astounded at the man's impudence, but within seconds the duke was outside, roaring for the other leaders to assemble.

"The first section has been attacked!" The word spread like wildfire. "The sultan laid an ambush for them and attacked this morning at sunrise!"

Count Garnier burst out of his tent and ran for his horse.

"To me, Theo!" he cried.

All over the camp, the morning routine was broken by shouts and roared commands. The knights and their mounted soldiers galloped off, leaving the foot soldiers and archers to follow at a double-march behind. The rest of the camp was in total confusion.

Theo rode at Count Garnier's right hand. Gritting his teeth against the bone-shattering pounding of Centurion's hooves, he checked that his sword was holstered securely, readjusted his dagger and settled his shield more firmly into his left shoulder. At last! The blood sang through his veins.

Godfrey and Hugh of Vermandois led. When they slowed down to give the chargers a rest, the horses, as frenzied as the knights themselves, tossed their manes, rolled their eyes wildly and tore at their bits.

It seemed to take forever to negotiate the last pass through the hills above Dorylaeum, but finally they burst out onto the plain above the city. Below them, they could see the embattled crusaders. They had formed a circle, with the non-combatant pilgrims in the center. Women were carrying water from springs to where the wounded were lying. The camp was surrounded by the Turks. As Godfrey drew his army up into position, Theo could see Turkish archers run in a line to the front of their soldiers, discharge their arrows into the ring of defending crusaders and then quickly retreat behind their own men to reload. Another line rushed to take their place. A ceaseless rain of arrows shot into the crusaders, making it impossible for them to advance and fight the Turks hand to hand.

"A cowardly way to wage war," Aimery raged, beside Theo.

"Cowardly perhaps, but very effective," Theo replied grimly.

Even as they watched, knights fell and horses crashed to the ground. Earsplitting battlecries from the triumphant Turks reached Theo's ears. Then Godfrey's own trumpets sounded out.

"Charge!" The cry rang out all along the lines. Bohemond, Robert of Normandy and Stephen of Blois led their men on the left flank. Raymond of Toulouse and Robert of Flanders took the center. Count Garnier, with Theo close beside him, followed Godfrey and Hugh on the right. There was no time for fear; Theo drew his sword, and they were upon the enemy.

In an instant, Theo's world became a howling hell of clashing weapons. A blow landed on his shield, almost knocking him from his saddle. Before he could recover, a scimitar from the side caught his helmet with a crack that sent a ringing right through his brain. Everything went red before him. He reeled in the saddle.

So soon? he thought, desperate. Am I to die so soon? Before I have even struck a blow? Anger swept his mind and his vision cleared. The noise around him disappeared. He was alone in his own silence. A figure loomed up before him, turban flaming in the sun, scimitar raised. Theo slashed with his sword and felt the sudden shock as the blade sank deep into flesh. He yanked it out, even as he was wheeling Centurion to meet another figure on his right. He thrust backhanded at the man, and caught him in the side. The man fell, but Theo was already past him and joined with another. Thrust, cut, parry. Thrust again. Theo fought in a frenzy. When trumpets sounded again, they seemed to belong to another world. It wasn't until he found himself charging after a horseman and realized the Turks were retreating, that he came back to the reality of where he was.

✝   ✝   ✝

"It was Adhemar, Bishop of Le Puy, who saved us," Amalric gasped, grunting with pain as a servant doused his leg with water. A scimitar had ripped open his old boar wound. "He's a clever tactician for a churchman. Bribed guides to take him over the hills behind the Turks and fell on them from the rear. They broke as soon as he attacked."

The crusaders had regrouped to tend to their injuries. Theo had found Amalric, although he couldn't, at the moment, remember how. Amalric's words came to him as though from a vast distance. He stared at blood flowing down his own right arm, and wondered stupidly where it was coming from.

EIGHT

The army rested at Dorylaeum for two days to recover from the battle. It had been an enormous victory, and the sultan was in full retreat, but there had been many losses and the crusaders felt a new respect for the Turks as soldiers. Tancred and Bohemond's own brother William had been slain. Fortunately, Theo's wound was slight.

The general mood within the camp, however, was one of elation. In their flight, the Turks had left behind their tents to be overrun by the crusaders. At last, the booty they had wished for so eagerly was theirs. The sultan had carried a good part of his treasure with him, and the crusaders were quick to plunder it. They captured many fine horses, too, and some other animals that Theo had never seen before. Tall, gangling, sandy-colored beasts, they had long, ugly faces with a decidedly insolent look to them. What amazed Theo most of all, however, were the humps on their rough-coated backs that swayed when they moved. They walked with a lolling, lumbering gait, on splayed hooves at the end of thin, ungainly legs. Theo could never have imagined more unlikely animals.

When Godfrey called a general conference of his leaders and their knights to plan the next stages of the march, Theo accompanied Count Garnier. The count had praised him for his conduct during the battle, and Theo's heart was light as he strode beside his foster father to the duke's tent. He had fought, finally, and he had fought well. He had a right to feel proud. But, deep inside, something lurked. He could not forget the feeling of his sword sinking into flesh for the first time, and the flash of the eyes beneath the crimson turban as the man attacking him realized he had been mortally wounded. The memory made Theo uneasy, and he did not want to examine it. Each time it recurred, he thrust it back down and thought of other things.

"We keep together from now on. There will be no repeat of the ambush at Dorylaeum." Duke Godfrey's voice rang out as they entered.

"We will march along the edge of the mountains. The going will be hard, but Taticius has assured me that there are Christian villages along the way, fertile fields and many good wells. Provisions should not be a problem."

A murmur arose, an undercurrent of suspicion, at the name of the emperor's engineer.

"Taticius knows the route. He will guide us." Godfrey's tone of voice quelled any argument; the murmuring ceased.

The sun was high and the early July heat already almost unbearable when the crusading army set out yet again. The mountains to the south of them looked coolly inviting and green, but the winds that blew off the wide, seemingly endless salt marshes to the north were arid and dry. Never had Theo seen such a bleak land. They were well provisioned, however, and carried a more than ample supply of water that easily lasted until they reached Pisidian Antioch. The town was peaceful, its leaders eager to provide the crusaders with supplies. Spirits rose in spite of the heat, which was increasing daily.

Once they had left the town's shelter, however, conditions deteriorated quickly. The heavily armed knights and foot soldiers began to suffer in the heat, and they drank recklessly, heedless of the need to ration. Water quickly became scarce. At Philomelium, they were able to take on a little more, but not nearly enough, and the country beyond this city became more and more desolate.

On the third day out of Philomelium, the vanguard of the army spotted a village. Word spread back quickly. They would be able to reprovision here, and supply themselves with badly needed water. The knights spurred their horses forward eagerly. Theo rode with Amalric at the very front. His mouth was dry and parched; the horse he rode wheezed and heaved with thirst beneath him. He saw the trees waving above the low village walls and licked his cracked lips in anticipation. He could almost taste the cool velvet of the water.

"It is very quiet," Amalric said.

The knights around them, who had been calling out in their excitement, fell silent, one by one.

None of the noise and bustle of a normal village welcomed them. No dog barked at their approach, no chickens scrabbled in the dust, no goats nibbled at the stunted bushes by the roadside. The surrounding fields, which should have been heavy with grain, were overgrown and wild. And nowhere was there any sign of human life. Not an adult, not a child.

The gates of the village hung wide open, askew. As they filed through, a sight of complete destruction met their eyes. Houses were burned, walls tumbled down. The streets were strewn with refuse. In the center of the village, a bridge over a dried-up stream had fallen, or been destroyed. The wind soughed between the abandoned buildings. It looked as if all life here had ceased years ago.

Godfrey drew up beside the large cistern at the town center. He stared down into it, then raised his eyes to the men watching him.

"Sand. It is filled with sand."

✝   ✝   ✝

So it was with every village they came to and every well they found. The men suspected treason and were quick to blame Taticius and the Greek guides, but Alexius's men were suffering equally. They had had no way of knowing that drought, years of warfare and Turkish invasions had reduced the countryside to a wasteland since they had last traveled this way. The army trudged on. The horses' hooves turned up stones from the rocky beds of parched streams. There was no water anywhere. Every cistern they found along the way was dry. Theo saw men, in their desperation, ripping off branches of thorn bushes and chewing them in a vain attempt to find moisture. Theo rationed the pitiful amount of water he had left carefully, using it only to wet his lips and tongue whenever the thirst became unbearable. Then, even that was gone. He tore off a thorn branch himself to chew, but threw it away in disgust when the dryness of it made his torment worse. His tongue swelled within his mouth until he could hardly speak. And always, the sun beat down upon them mercilessly, causing them to sweat and lose even more precious moisture from their bodies.

Horses were the first to perish. Theo worried about Centurion, who was in great distress. He set William to gathering the prickly plants that grew along the way, and rubbed them between his hands to provide fodder for the horse. By the time they made camp at night, Centurion was covered in sweat and would hardly eat. He grew weak, and faltered during the long daily marches. Knights whose horses died were forced to go on foot. Poorly shod for walking on such stony roads, their feet soon became sore and inflamed. Sheep, goats and dogs were used to pull the baggage trains. The camels, the strange beasts captured from the Turks, fared the best. They seemed to be able to trudge on, unmindful of the heat, and not bothered in the least by the lack of water. They were useful as beasts of burden, but cursed with ugly tempers and liable to bite. They could also spit a slimy, noxious stream a surprising distance, as more than one groom found out.

"How are you?" Theo asked Emma as she appeared on her mare beside him early one morning. Her face was gaunt, her eyes enormous in her face.

"I am well enough," she said. She, too, seemed to have trouble speaking. "But the children are suffering." She brushed a tangled strand of greasy hair out of her eyes. "How much longer will this go on, do you think?"

"Iconium is two days' march from here," Theo answered. His brow furrowed. In spite of what she said, she did not look well. "It is a large town," he went on, trying to sound reassuring, but a note of bitterness crept into his voice. "Well provisioned, Taticius says. There are streams in the valley of Meran behind the city that cannot run dry, he tells us. But he has been wrong every step of the way up until now. And we do not know whether the Turks have taken the city. I do not think we have the strength to fight for it if they have." He turned to look at the column strung out behind them. He could not see the pilgrims that followed at the very end, but he knew they straggled farther and farther behind every day; every night fewer of them made it into camp.

"What is to become of us, then?"

There was a quaver in Emma's voice that Theo had not heard before. It shocked him into looking at her more carefully. He saw then how thin her wrists were, and how bony the slender fingers had become. He looked at his own hands and realized for the first time that they, too, were lean and sinewy, roped with veins like an old man's. Without thinking, he reached out to her.

Her fingers tightened around his as he grasped her hand. She met his eyes and drew a deep breath. She straightened in her saddle. Then she gave a small nod, as if to reassure him, or herself. Or perhaps both of them.

Two days later, toward the middle of August, almost a year to the day since Godfrey's crusade had left the Ardennes, they reached Iconium. The city lay in a now familiar, deserted silence as they rode toward it. The heat rose in shimmering waves. There were signs that the Turks had, indeed, occupied it, but they must have fled at the coming of the crusaders.

Theo's heart sank. Then a joyous shout from the knights in the lead sent a thrill of hope through him, and he spurred his horse forward eagerly. A well lay just within the gates. Knights were kneeling beside it, scooping clear, sparkling water out in great handfuls. Theo raised his eyes to the hills beyond. Streams glinted and tumbled down the slopes between rows and rows of carefully tended orchards. Taticius had finally been right.

✝   ✝   ✝

Count Garnier set up his camp across a swiftly flowing stream from Duke Godfrey's. Theo's tent lay under a grove of trees whose leaves filtered out the harsh sun. Within a day, he had forgotten what thirst was like. Centurion spent the first twenty-four hours planted in the river, then began to graze without stopping. The news that they would rest there for several more days restored the spirits of all the crusaders. When Amalric burst in upon Theo to invite him on a bear hunt in the foothills, Theo accepted with alacrity.

The duke himself led the party, but Theo's enthusiasm was checked when he saw Guy. During the past few months, while they had been on the road, it had been easy to avoid him. Now, however, there was no escaping the confrontation. Guy drew his horse up sharply when he saw Theo.

"So." The word was a sneer. "You will have better luck keeping to your own game today, I hope."

A sharp answer rose to Theo's lips, but he bit it back. The day was too fine and the relief from the harshness of the road too great to spoil with arguments. He forced a nod and determined to keep out of Guy's way.

Beyond the shelter of the valley, the land became more densely wooded and rose gently toward the mountains. A pack of dogs had been let loose and were loping ahead of the knights, casting about for the scent of game. All of a sudden, one caught it. A nose was thrust skyward and the hound howled to the heavens above. Another animal took up the scent, and then another. Howls turned into frenzied barking, and the pack headed into the forest. Theo spurred his horse on. The animal, startled, gave a great leap forward and they were off at a gallop.

As soon as they entered the trees, they were forced to rein their mounts in. Soon the bush became too thick for riding, even at a walk. Tossing their horses' reins to their grooms, the knights dismounted and began to thread their way through, the hounds' belling drawing them on.

"There! Do you hear it? They have caught up to their prey!" Amalric shouted, at Theo's shoulder.

The dogs' crying had changed in note and tone; the barks had become frantic.

"On!" Godfrey cried, and drew his sword. Footmen fanned out as best they could on either side, their halberds and spears hampering them in the dense underbrush. The dogs' noise grew closer.

Sweat poured into Theo's eyes, but he was hardly aware of it. He drew his sword and beat back the low-hanging branches of the trees. Without warning, he stumbled into a clearing. The dogs were circling a tree, leaping and snarling. Theo looked up. There, in its branches, dark against the dark background of the forest, was a bear. Theo caught his breath at the size of it. Even from where he stood, it looked larger than any animal he had ever seen. A rank smell hit his nostrils. The bear did not seem frightened. Its eyes, small in the enormous head, were fixed on the mad animals beneath it with what seemed to be contempt.

"Call off the dogs!" The duke's order rang out, but the dogs were beyond hearing, let alone obeying. Two of the animal trainers stepped forward with whips and began laying about them in the pack. Godfrey moved forward impatiently, hitting at the nearest hound with the flat of his sword. At that instant, the bear jumped.

As the huge animal hurtled out of the branches above him, Godfrey threw himself to one side. The bear landed a sword's length away from him. It hesitated for a moment, as if confused, turned toward the prostrate duke and raised itself up on its hind legs to its full height. Godfrey was on his feet in an instant. His sword flashed. At the same moment, every man in the party surged forward. The closest to the duke was Guy. He slashed at the bear with his sword and hit it on the shoulder, drawing blood. The bear whirled, unbelievably graceful for a creature of its size. Godfrey took advantage of its movement to thrust with his sword, and the blade sank deep into its side. The bear whirled back and, with one swipe of its forepaw, sent Godfrey spinning. Guy struck again. Theo and Amalric closed in beside him, adding their blows to his. The bear roared and lashed out with first one, and then the other of its massive paws. Theo had an overwhelming impression of teeth, the flying froth of saliva and a red, cavernous mouth. The bear's roar paralyzed him for an instant, and then he struck again. Another blow from the bear's paw felled Guy. He lay, stunned, as the bear turned toward him. Theo took a step forward and straddled the fallen knight, protecting him. With his sword, he struck the bear just above its eyes. The animal lunged for him. At that moment, a spear hurled by one of Godfrey's men whistled past Theo's shoulder and buried itself deep in the animal's chest. For a moment, everything seemed to stop. The bear stood, immobile. As Theo drew back his arm to strike again, the animal crumpled to the ground.

Blood was everywhere. Guy groaned, then raised himself to his knees and shook his head as Theo stepped back from him. Duke Godfrey lay ominously still. His men ran to him. It was impossible to tell how much of the blood on him and around him was his, and how much was the bear's. Amalric and the rest of his party slid a cloak under the duke and raised him carefully. Guy stood for a second, still trying to clear his head. He looked at Theo. For a minute, Theo thought he was going to say something, but then he shook his head again and joined the party of men carrying the duke.

† † †

There was feasting that night in Godfrey's camp. Great chunks of bear roasted over every fire. Godfrey was not seriously injured, although his wounds were substantial. The bear's claws had raked his chest in deep grooves. A healer had bound the gashes as well as he could, but the duke was too weak and in too much pain to participate in the celebration. Theo and Amalric, however, wolfed down their share of the hot, greasy meat. When he had stuffed himself to the point of nausea, Theo tossed his last bone to the hounds that skulked around their feet, and sank back beside the fire with a sigh of contentment. As he did so, he caught sight of Guy sitting on the other side, glaring at him through the firelight.

"Guy does not look overly grateful for the favor I did him today," Theo said to Amalric, trying to make his voice light.

"It was the worst thing you could have done," Amalric replied. He wiped the grease from his chin. "He is a twisted sort. I truly think he would rather have died than have you save him."

Nine

They took water with them when they left
Iconium, well rested and eager once again,
but the valley through which they now traveled was fertile and flowing with streams. Almost at
once, they ran into a Turkish army led by the Emir
Hassan. Bohemond led the attack and the outnumbered Turks retreated without resistance. The crusaders fired off a comet that night in celebration. Theo
and Amalric watched it streak through the blackness,
shedding sparks.

116

"An omen," Amalric said. "We shall have nothing but victories from now on."

And so it seemed. As the summer wore on, the crusaders forged ahead, defeating the Turkish troops wherever they encountered them. They followed the road through Caesarea, but Baldwin, with some of the Flemish knights and the Lorrainers, split from the main party and crossed into Cilicia.

"He's after more gains for himself, of course," was Emma's scornful comment. "It galls him to share his spoils with all the rest of the crusaders."

"How do you and Lady Godvere manage without him?" Theo asked.

"Perfectly well," Emma retorted. "We have the servants to help us, and a groom. It is a relief not to have him around."

By the end of September, with the summer heat abating somewhat, they reached Caesarea to find it deserted by the Turks.

"Our good fortune holds," Theo remarked one evening, sitting by the campfire with Amalric.

"Good fortune has nothing to do with it," Amalric responded. "We are invincible. Nothing can stand in our way."

Theo laughed. The battles they had fought together had forged their friendship fast. There was, however, one great difference between them. After each battle, the blood lust lived on in Amalric until he had worked it out with riotous celebration. In this, he was like most of the other men. With Theo, it was different. In the wildness of battle, he was one with Amalric, but when the fighting was over, there was always a time of sickness. A time during which he had to be alone. Amalric could not understand. He had teased, cajoled and even tried to shame Theo into joining the carousing that followed each battle, but to no avail. Finally, he had shrugged his shoulders and given up.

"I know you are among the bravest of us all," he said. "You should be one of the most eager to make merry."

"I cannot explain it," was Theo's only response, and Amalric was finally forced to relent. To Theo himself, his sickness after battles was a gnawing, secret worry.

In October, the rains began. The mountains they had been following now loomed ahead of them, their towering peaks already snow-capped. They rose to heights higher than many had seen before.

"We are to cross *those*?" For once, Amalric seemed taken aback as Theo drew up beside him and they paused to contemplate what lay before them.

"So it would seem," Theo answered.

The way they followed could not really be called a road. It quickly turned into no more than a muddy path that led up steep inclines and skirted terrifying precipices. As they climbed higher, the mud became icy. The pilgrims shivered and slipped on the treacherous slopes. No one dared to ride. First one horse slipped and fell over the edge, then another, and yet another. A whole line of baggage animals, roped together, fell and dragged each other down into the abyss that yawned at their side. Heavily armored knights began to unburden themselves. At first, they offered their arms and equipment for sale to any who would buy. Then, in desperation, as the way grew ever steeper, some merely threw them away. Men following behind could pick up whatever they wished, but few did. It was only too apparent that the more lightly they traveled, the better were their chances.

"These mountains are cursed!" The words were muttered up and down the line, and indeed the crusaders were losing more men through accidents than they had in all the battles so far. The pilgrims at the end of the procession fared even worse. Carts and wagons were either abandoned or lost to the depths below; people kept only what they could carry on their backs. There was no stopping, not even for a rest; the rain was fast turning to sleet, and snow was on the way. They had to make the crossing before it came.

Theo led Centurion, leaving William to deal with the palfrey and the groom's own nag. He had fastened his weapons and his chain mail onto the charger's saddle. If Centurion slipped and was lost, lost as well would be all that Theo owned; but Centurion was proving to be amazingly sure-footed in his own heavy, plodding way. Suddenly, Theo heard a cry behind him. He turned just in time to see the hindquarters of

William's nag sag beneath him and slide over the edge of the path. To his horror, Theo saw that William had, against all advice, mounted the horse. The groom had complained unendingly about the need to walk ever since the climb had begun and, it would seem, had at last given in to the temptation to ride. Before Theo could move, the horse tumbled off the edge of the precipice. William uttered one short scream, and then there was silence. Appalled, Theo looked over the edge, but thick trees below masked any sign of horse or rider. Theo's palfrey, reins trailing, stood listlessly at the spot where William had gone over. Theo had no time to try to see any farther. The horse was blocking the trail; men and animals on the path below were beginning to back up.

"Move on up there!" a rough voice shouted. "No stopping on the trail!"

Theo reached over, grabbed the palfrey's reins and moved forward, leading the two animals. It had all happened so suddenly. He bowed his head into the driving sleet and urged the horses on. He had not liked William very much, but they had marched together, shared meals together for over a year now. It was unthinkable that he could be gone—that from one moment to the next, he could just cease to exist.

Theo stumbled and caught himself just as one foot slipped toward the edge of the path. Centurion snorted as if indignant at his clumsiness. Theo shook the rain out of his eyes and focused all his senses on the task of leading the two horses safely. Finally, the path evened out and they began to descend.

On a wet, cold afternoon, just before darkness overtook them, the leading knights and their entourages emerged from the pass into the valley that surrounded Marash. The Armenian population there, under their prince, Thatoul, came out to meet them in a joyous welcome. As he tethered the horses and unpacked his tent, Theo looked back at the mountains. Streams of exhausted pilgrims still trickled down to the plain below where tents were starting to rise and fires starting to flicker. Hundreds more were on the crossing behind them. Night was falling fast, and the sleet had turned to snow. He could see it driving whitely across the dark trees on the mountainside. Theo's breath steamed into the wintry air. He rubbed his chilled hands together to warm them. How many more would perish before they reached this side of the mountains?

As soon as he could, Theo searched out Baldwin's camp. He was worried about Emma. How had she and the Lady Godvere survived the crossing? As he approached their tents, he heard the sounds of a child wailing, a high-pitched, keening noise that seemed to go on and on. He was surprised to see no sign of a fire.

"Emma?" he called out. When there was no answer, he made for the tent where the child was crying.

As he pulled open the flap, he gasped, and drew back at the smell. Then he took a deep breath and pushed his way in. The two boys lay on blankets. Beside them, the girl sat, hair tangled over her face and down her shoulders, wailing. Godvere lay on another blanket, breathing heavily; her wide, flat face shone with sweat. Emma knelt, bathing her forehead with a rag soaked in water. She looked up as Theo came in.

"What has happened?" Theo asked.

"They are all ill. Godvere is the sickest right now, although the children are worsening quickly. They took a chill during the crossing and are now all burning with fever."

"And you?"

"I am well, thanks be to God. But the crossing was terrible. We lost our wagon."

"Why do you not have a fire? Where are the servants?"

Emma shrugged. "I know not. One perished when the wagon went over. The others disappeared as soon as my lady and the children took ill. Our groom helped to raise the tents, and then he also left. I think they fear the fever."

"Have you eaten?"

"There has not been time."

"I'll make a fire for you. Do you have food for a broth?"

"Yes. A woman was here from the village. A kind woman. She brought vegetables and bread, but she wouldn't stay. She, too, was afraid." Emma gestured toward a basket by the door flap.

"I'll make a soup for you, then."

"You cannot . . ."

"I most certainly can. I am an excellent cook. It was necessary to learn rather than eat the messes William prepared—" He stopped. William's cry echoed again in his mind.

Within the hour, he had made a nourishing soup, supplementing it with meat from his own stores. He brought a bowl in to Emma and helped her feed it to the children. The boys were too weak to take more than a few sips. The girl drank greedily, then fell into a heavy sleep that was more like a stupor. They could not raise Godvere sufficiently to get her to taste even a mouthful. Her breathing was rapidly getting more labored, and her breath was foul. Each snoring breath was followed by a lull that threatened to be her last.

"They have sent to Cilicia for Lord Baldwin," Emma said when they had done what they could for Godvere and the children, and were sitting together beside the fire. Emma held a bowl thick with vegetables and meat in her hands. As she ate, color began to come back to her pale, drawn face. "But he is busy conquering territory to lay up for himself, I hear, and I would not be surprised if he did not bother to come." She looked at the bowl of soup in her hands, then back up at Theo. "I thank you, Theo," she said. "You are a good friend to me. My only friend here, I fear."

Friend. As Theo looked at Emma, he knew that what he felt for her was much more than friendship.

Baldwin did come, but only in time to watch his wife die. The children followed soon after. Theo saw him standing, tall and sombre, beside their gravesides as the priests said mass over them. Emma stood slightly behind him. As Theo watched, Baldwin turned to her and said something. They were too far away for Theo to make out the words, but he saw a quick flush rise to Emma's cheeks.

The next morning, he hurried over to Baldwin's camp, determined to talk to Emma. Now that Godvere and the children were gone, he feared for her safety alone with that man. When he walked into the clearing where the tents had been, however, they were gone. He stopped, shocked and uncomprehending for a moment, then raced to Godfrey's encampment.

"My Lord Baldwin," he gasped out to the first sentry he came upon. "Know you where he is?"

"He and all his entourage left with the first light," the man replied. "Stricken with grief over the death of his lady and children, no doubt." Sarcasm lay heavy over the words.

"Where did they go?"

The guard looked at Theo, surprised at the intensity of his questioning.

"To the east, where there is more to be gained, rumors say. He is more anxious to carve out his own kingdom, I am told, than to remain with the crusade." As if suddenly aware that he was speaking unwisely, the guard snapped his mouth shut and would say no more.

Theo turned away, a sickness in his stomach. What about Emma? For a moment, he thought wildly about saddling Centurion and riding after them, but even as the thought formed itself, he heard the trumpets sounding and the bugles calling. They were to march today—on to Antioch.

† † †

Theo saddled his palfrey and made Centurion ready for the trip without any awareness of what he was doing. His mind was reeling. It was inconceivable that Emma should disappear from his life in such a manner. It was impossible! And with Baldwin . . . He hadn't the slightest doubt about the treatment she would receive at his hands. Why had she gone? Why hadn't she at least contrived to tell him she was going and to say farewell? Didn't she care for him at all? She had called him friend—even if she felt no more than that, how could she have left him in such a way?

He finished his preparations, swung into the saddle and rode to join his foster father. To the east, the guard had said. He scanned the horizon. Where in the east? Where had she gone?

"Why so glum, my son?" the count asked as he rode up. "Are you not excited? Once we liberate Antioch, the way southward to the Holy Land will be open to us. Our journey goes well!"

Theo didn't answer. He swung his horse alongside

125

the count as they took their places in the train. Centurion stomped behind on a lead rope that Theo held loosely in one hand.

"We must see about finding you another groom," the count said as Centurion edged forward and irritably tried to shoulder Garnier's horse out of the way. The slight nudge was powerful enough to cause the animal to stagger off the path. The count gathered his reins and brought his horse back to Theo's side with difficulty. It eyed Centurion nervously. Centurion bared his teeth and tried to nip the unfortunate animal's flank. Theo only just managed to haul on the lead rope and forestall him.

"I'm sorry for poor William, but he must be replaced," the count said. "That warhorse of yours is a menace."

"He dislikes sharing the path," Theo said, but his mind was not on the horse. He rode in silence for a while, but finally could keep quiet no longer.

"Know you where went Baldwin, my lord?" he asked.

Count Garnier's mouth twisted and his normally open face closed. "Tarsus, the rumor is. He wants the city for himself. Bohemond has sent a troop of Normans after him to keep control in crusader hands." He paused for a moment. "It seems sometimes there is more fighting and jealousy among ourselves than between us and the enemy. It is disheartening."

When they camped that night, Theo refused Amalric's offer to drink and make merry at his campsite.

"There are wenches galore who will make you forget that little servant girl of Godvere's instantly," Amalric teased.

Theo flushed. "I had not given her a thought," he snapped. "I was hardly even aware she had gone."

"And is that why you have been so intent on discovering Baldwin's whereabouts?"

Theo turned abruptly and left.

He boiled water for soup, threw in a few turnips and a bone with meat on it, and then just sat, staring into the flames. He had no appetite for food. A rustle in the bushes startled him into awareness.

"Who goes there?" he demanded, springing to his feet.

A figure emerged, leading a decrepit nag. It was a young boy, hair chopped off short in the Norman fashion. In the gathering darkness, Theo had difficulty making out his features.

"You are in need of a groom, my lord?" the boy said.

At the sound of the words, Theo's heart took a great leap. For a moment, he couldn't speak. Then he found his tongue.

"Emma?" It was barely a whisper. "Come closer to the fire!"

The figure emerged into the flame's light. Theo looked at him incredulously. The boy bore a slight resemblance to the girl, but the short hair changed the look of the face completely. He was dressed in a belted tunic and leggings; a small dagger such as the servants carried was tucked in at his waist.

"Emma?" Theo repeated, not daring to breathe.

The boy smiled, and in that instant became recognizable.

"Emma! What are you doing here? And in that garb?"

"You need a groom, do you not? Then, I am here to be your groom."

Iconium

ARMENIAN STATES

Antioch

MEDITERRANEAN SEA

Ten

"Impossible!"

"Why?" Emma was defiant.

"Because . . . because you'll be recognized."

"Not now that my lord Baldwin's gone. No one else in the camp except you knows me well, and even you didn't recognize me until I spoke. I'll just not talk when others are around."

"It can't possibly work. Besides, you can't be a groom!"

"It *can* work. I've given it thought. And why could

I not be a groom? I know much about horses. At home, I helped my father many a time. What I don't know, you can teach me."

"But why, Emma? Why do you want to do this?"

Her brows drew together. Her mouth set. "I do not want to be with Baldwin now that my lady is no longer alive. I am not really his servant. You said so yourself. I have the right to do as I wish."

"But to travel with me as my groom—it is impossible!" Theo repeated. He realized he was blustering.

"Do you not want me here?" Emma's chin tilted. "Would you rather that I traveled with Lord Baldwin?"

"No, of course not! I trust the man not at all and I am very glad you are not with him." Theo stopped short. The fact that Emma had *not* gone with Baldwin finally sank in, and a singing lightness began to bubble up through his veins.

"I got the clothes from a groom who was anxious to rid himself of extra weight on the trek over the mountains. I thought they might be useful, although at the time I wasn't really certain what for. It was good I did so, though, wasn't it?"

The situation was impossible. What would the count say if he found out? He would send her back to Baldwin, of course. One thought after another tumbled into Theo's mind. But over all the joy within him rose, and in spite of himself he broke into a broad smile.

"You make a comely lad, I must say," he said.

Emma answered his smile with one of her own.

"The night before my lord Baldwin left, I stole the least of his horses, snuck out of his camp and have been trailing you ever since." She sounded extremely pleased with herself.

"So, a horse thief as well."

"I brought a mule with me when I joined Lady Godvere," Emma answered quickly. "Baldwin has the better bargain, for it was a far better animal than this nag, but I dared not steal the mule back, nor take the sweet mare I usually rode, which belonged to my lord. This half-dead beast will not even be missed." She looked full at Theo. The smile died and her face became serious once more. "I cannot come back to this crusade if you do not take me in, Theo. A woman alone . . . It is not possible. I would have to return to Baldwin." Her hands clenched into fists at her sides. She took a deep breath. "May I stay? May I be your groom?"

"I know not how . . . If anyone should find out—"

"I have thought that out, too," she broke in. "Say I am an Armenian, from one of the villages we passed through. That I wished to join the crusade. And say that I am a mute. Then I need not speak at all. My voice is most likely to give me away." She stopped.

"I have a small tent that William used," Theo said slowly, getting used to the idea. "You could have that. It would be best if you always set it up close to mine. You would have to avoid the other grooms—they will think you strange for doing so, but you must not let them get too close to you."

"Strange they may think me, and strange I will be." She bit her lip and looked down at the fire, then raised her eyes back to Theo. "You understand, Theo, that I will be your groom. Nothing else."

Theo felt the blood rising to his cheeks. "Of course." The words came out more brusquely than he had intended.

"I did not mean to insult you," Emma said. "It was just . . . I had to make it clear."

"Of course," Theo repeated stiffly. "I would never have thought of anything else." But the racing of his blood belied his words.

She had been facing Theo rigidly, her whole body immobile and tense. Now, suddenly, she relaxed.

"So," she said, "I will go to war after all." Her lips curled in a smile of pure satisfaction. "And as a man, not a mewling maid."

"Grooms do not make war any more than women do," Theo said. The words came out even more stiffly.

"Perhaps not," Emma replied. "But I will be at the front, not the back. And I will be helping you prepare for your battles. It will be almost as good. Now, where is that tent?"

† † †

"You have a new groom, I see," Amalric said as he rode up beside Theo a few days later. He was munching on one of the small, purplish fruits that the people in these parts loved.

The way was along level plains and the riding was easy. Once through the mountains, the rains had ceased and the cool autumn weather was a relief to them all. Amalric held out one of the figs, as they were called, to Theo. Theo took it, and used the opportunity of splitting it and squeezing the soft, sweet, seed-filled pulp into his mouth to marshal his thoughts. Emma rode discreetly behind, leading Centurion. She had found a loosely woven hood somewhere and wore it constantly, far down over her eyes. No one tried to ride near her. The other grooms had learned to give Centurion plenty of space and their horses knew well enough not to get within his reach. Centurion, however, was behaving himself admirably. He had taken to Emma immediately, and followed wherever she led him as docilely as a pup.

"My groom says he is none too sociable. Keeps to himself."

"He is mute," Theo answered quickly.

"How came you by him, then?" Amalric asked. He seemed only moderately curious, making conversation merely to help ease his impatience. His eyes searched the road ahead of them as if willing the walls of Antioch to come into view.

"He appeared in my camp one evening," Theo answered, casting a quick, nervous glance at his friend. He had considered telling Amalric about Emma, but had decided against it. He was not altogether sure how Amalric would react. At the very least, he would laugh, and he would certainly think Theo was mad. "He is from one of the Armenian villages. He understands a little of our language and managed to make me know that he wanted to join the crusade. I thought he might do as my groom."

Amalric was only half listening.

"Good fortune for you," he answered, but clearly his thoughts were elsewhere. "We should arrive at the gates of Antioch in a few days' time." He threw the fig skin to one side. "What shall we find there, I wonder?"

† † †

What they found were fortifications that exceeded all imagining. They had a skirmish at the Iron Bridge that crossed the Orontes River but, after a sharp struggle, the army of Bishop Adhemar defeated the Turks who were defending it, and led the way across. Once past that barrier, the crusaders followed the river until, after a sharp bend, the walls of Antioch suddenly appeared ahead. Theo, riding with Amalric, drew in his breath.

On their right-hand side, to the north, the wall rose out of the low, marshy ground along the river, solid and formidable. Directly ahead, the massive fortifications towered above them. On their left, to the south, the wall followed steeply up the slopes of a mountain, then over the summit and out of sight on the far side.

All along, at regular intervals, towers were built so that every meter of wall was within bowshot of one of them. At the very peak of the mountain, within the southern wall, a stone citadel stood guard, with the flag of the Turkish governor of the city, Yaghi-Siyan, flying defiantly above it. The crusaders could see that the citadel, walls and towers were heavily manned, but there was no sign of soldiers.

"He knows we are here," Amalric muttered. "Does he have such contempt for us that he does not even bother to put his army on display?"

The city of Antioch spread itself out within these fortifications. From where he was, Theo could see houses, villas and palaces dotting the hillsides above him. Gardens stretched out luxuriously. The climate was so much milder here than in the north that they were still filled with flowers and trees in full leaf. Smoke rose from innumerable cooking fires, and the heavy scent of spices wafted down to them.

With a flourish of trumpets, the crusading army advanced. Theo could not tear his eyes away from the sight of the magnificent city sprawled out behind its walls on the mountainside before him. But something was wrong. It took him several moments to realize that, beyond the noise that surrounded him—the blaring of horns and trumpets, the neighing of horses, the shouting of men and the usual crash of arms as the foot soldiers followed—there was no sound. The city was silent. He could see no one on the streets, in the gardens or around the houses. The people were keeping themselves out of sight. Waiting.

Godfrey signaled to his followers to halt, as Bohemond and the other leaders spread out along the wall toward the mountain. It was immediately obvious that they could not surround the city as they had Nicaea. It was also immediately obvious that taking Nicaea had been child's play compared to the battle ahead. And yet, Antioch had to be defeated; take it they must. If they left it as a Turkish bastion, they were leaving themselves open to attack from behind as they continued on to Jerusalem.

Besides, Antioch was one of the most important Christian cities. St. Peter had preached here, and the followers of Christ had been proclaimed "Christians" for the first time within these walls. There was still a large Christian community in the city, led by a patriarch of the church. It was imperative that they reclaim Antioch. But, looking at those massive, silent fortifications, Theo felt a creeping doubt within him. How was this to be done? He settled himself deeper into his saddle and stared at the city before him. Even Amalric had fallen silent.

Godfrey's army was deployed around the northern gate, on level ground with the Orontes River behind it. Bohemond took up a key position facing the eastern gate on the road they had taken from the Iron Bridge. They guessed that reinforcements for the city, if any were needed, would come this way. Robert of Flanders and Stephen of Blois watched over the remaining gate on this side, flanked by Raymond of Toulouse and Bishop Adhemar. There were two other gates, one that faced west, and the main river gate where a stone bridge crossed the Orontes; but the crusaders did not have enough men to guard them as well. This meant that the Turks within the city still had access to the western road that led to the sea.

"This siege will be a long one, my son," Count Garnier said, as they set up their tents.

† † †

At first, the footsore crusaders settled down with relief. As October passed into November and the weather became even cooler, they were grateful for the rest. The surroundings of Antioch were fertile and the vegetation abundant. There were fields of grain, grape vines everywhere, and trees bent down with the weight of oranges, lemons, figs and other fruit. Herds of cattle roamed freely; the soldiers killed them indiscriminately and ate only the choicest cuts of meat, throwing away the rest to the dogs. Horses grazed on what seemed to be limitless fodder. Every morning, the priests gave thanks for God's abundance and mercy. But within weeks, the thousands of hungry mouths had taken their toll, and detachments of the army had to be sent out to scavenge in the surrounding countryside. Still, no plans were made for storming the city.

"This cannot go on." Theo strode furiously into his campsite late one evening. "Our leaders wrangle among themselves and come to no decisions. And while we sit and do nothing, the Turks are brazenly going back and forth through the river gate and the western gate whenever they please." He paused. "What are you doing to that horse?"

Emma looked up from the shadows at the edge of the fire where she was tending Centurion. "Scratching his stomach," she answered complacently. "He loves a good belly tickle now and then." The hulking charger was standing with his head down, snuffling with contentment.

"He is a warhorse, not a puppy dog," Theo said irritably.

Emma quirked an eyebrow. She was about to make a sharp retort when a rustle in the bushes silenced her. Quickly, she lowered her head and drew her hood down over her eyes. She began to brush Centurion.

A figure stumbled out of the bushes.

"To me, Otto," he mumbled, voice sodden and blurry with drink. He staggered toward Emma.

"You are mistaken, sir," Theo said, advancing to ward him off. "This is not your camp."

"You! What are you doing here?" The figure straightened and glared at Theo.

With a shock, Theo recognized Guy.

"This is not your campsite," he repeated, his voice cold. "You are mistaken."

Guy stumbled over a root and fell flat. He reached out and grasped Emma's foot.

"You, boy, help me up," he commanded.

Emma wrested her foot from his grasp and stepped back.

"I said, help me!" Guy commanded. He got to his knees. Emma still made no move toward him.

"Is this how you train your minions?" Guy demanded, pulling himself up by Centurion's halter. The horse snorted, as if insulted, and side-stepped away from him. Guy swayed and caught Emma by the shoulder. She wrenched herself out of his grasp, sending him stumbling forward into Centurion's hindquarters. Centurion kicked out angrily, grazing Guy's shin. If the blow had landed squarely, it would have broken his leg.

With an oath, Guy swung out and hit Emma full across the side of the head. He raised his hand to strike again, but she was too quick for him. She dodged out of his reach, but in that second her hood fell back. For a moment, he stared at her, her face illuminated by the flickering firelight.

"You're pretty for a boy," he began, and then his brow furrowed. He shook his head as if trying to clear it. "Familiar," he muttered. "You look . . ."

Emma darted off into the darkness. Guy stood, still swaying, looking after her. He turned to Theo.

"Your groom has a familiar look to him. Where did you get him?" His speech was less slurred; the effort of thinking seemed to be clearing his head.

"He is Armenian, from Marash. There are many lads there who have his looks," Theo said quickly. He made a move toward Guy. "May I help you?" he asked, controlling his voice with an effort. It had taken all of his will not to lash out at Guy when he had struck Emma.

"I need no help from you," Guy retorted, drawing himself up. He took a step away from the campfire, and halted. He looked into the darkness where Emma had disappeared, then back at Theo. "There is something amiss here," he began. But the thickness was back in his voice. He shook his head again, passed his hand across his eyes and staggered away.

•Antioch

MEDITERRANEAN SEA

Eleven

"Siege engines, that's what we need. Good strong catapults to lob stones at the walls. You should advise Duke Godfrey to start building them at once. Ouch!"

"Hold still." Theo was bathing Emma's forehead where an angry, purple bruise was forming. "I do not *advise* the duke on anything. He does not listen to anyone as unimportant as I." Theo was fuming at Guy's cruelty, but knew there was nothing he could do. Knights cuffed grooms regularly. If he made any kind

141

of protest, he would only draw attention to Emma, and that he dared not do—especially since Guy had already sensed something unusual about her. Emma herself seemed to have taken the matter in her stride.

"And how does it come to pass that you consider yourself such an expert on war?" he asked, trying to keep his voice light.

"I have good ears. I listen."

"Perhaps the emperor will send us siege engines. He knows how things stand here and he is pledged to help us."

Emma snorted and tossed her head. The sodden cloth that Theo was using to bathe her forehead went flying.

"I wouldn't waste time waiting for his help," she said. "He hasn't done much for us so far. I think he is glad to see us gain back his lands for him, but he is not about to put himself in peril. That's what the talk around the campfires is, anyway. Perhaps my lord Raymond is right. He advocates attacking at once. God has protected us so far; surely he would give us victory over these heathen. It must gall Him immensely to see this holy city of His so desecrated."

"So now you speak for our Father Himself?" Theo cast a cautious glance around as he bent to retrieve the cloth. The talk verged on blasphemy. He quickly changed the subject. "You should not skulk around campfires. You might be discovered." Emma seemed to be getting more and more independent since transforming herself into a man, and worry made him sound like an over-anxious parent.

"How else should I know what is going on? I cannot converse with anyone or ask questions."

"I will tell you what you need to know." A mistake, and Theo realized it at once.

Emma arched an eyebrow, then winced. "It may be that you do not always know what *I* need to know."

Theo let out a grunt of exasperation. Living with Emma as his groom was presenting him with more complications than he had imagined. He was about to reply when yet another rustle in the bushes silenced him. He signaled to Emma and she quickly drew her hood back over her eyes. Theo turned toward the noise.

A man emerged. Theo reached for the dagger at his waist.

"Stay! Do not fear me! I am a Christian!" The man spoke the Frankish language of Godfrey and his people with difficulty.

"Who are you? Where are you from?" Theo's hand stayed on the haft of his weapon.

"From Antioch. Many of us have slipped out of the city this night. I have come with my wife and babe." He nodded to the shadows behind him, where Theo could just make out the figure of a woman holding a child in her arms.

"Take me to your lord, I pray you. I would speak with him."

"Your name?"

"Arnulf, my lord. Arnulf of Antioch."

Theo hesitated, then made his decision. "Come then. I will take you to my father, Count Garnier. But I warn you, if you mean any ill, he is well protected. You will not escape."

Not taking his eyes off the man, Theo reached out his right arm. Emma hastened to retrieve his sword from the tent and handed it to him. He buckled it on. As far as he could see, the man from Antioch was not armed, but Theo would take no chances.

He directed the way to the count's tent, keeping close behind Arnulf and his family. At the flap of the tent, he spoke to the halberdier on guard, a man Theo had known since his youth.

"I would speak with the count, Reynald. This man has something to say to him." He motioned to Arnulf to wait, then eased himself inside.

Count Garnier sat on a chest, a plank drawn up before him, supported by two other chests. He was peering at a crudely drawn map of the city of Antioch and its surroundings. He sat in a flickering pool of light given off by a burning wick floating in a dish of oil. The rest of the tent was in darkness. The smell of the lamp filled the tent, and smoke pricked at Theo's eyes. The count looked up as Theo came in.

"We must have a bridge of our own over this river if we are to receive any supplies from the coast," the count said. "What do you think, son, of building a bridge of boats?"

"Of boats?" Theo echoed, startled. "How could such a thing be done?" A bridge was necessary, he knew. The Orontes River ran from east to west at this point, and they were camped on the southern side of it, between it and the city walls. The only bridge across the river was at the western end of the city, where the Turks had control. The sea lay to the west, and the road to it was across the river. If the emperor did send supplies—*when* the emperor did send supplies, Theo corrected his thoughts immediately—there had to be a way across the river to the crusaders' encampments. But a bridge of boats? With a shake of his head, he brought his mind back to why he had come.

"There is a man outside, my lord. His name is Arnulf. He says he is a Christian from the city. He would like to speak with you."

Count Garnier looked up quickly. "Good!" he exclaimed. "News from within the walls would be invaluable. Bring him in, Theo, I would hear what he has to say, although I do not harbor much trust for these Byzantine Christians. They are a tricky lot. I have been warned."

Theo leaned out and signaled to the man. Arnulf slipped through the tent flap and stood before the count, head bowed. Even so, his hair brushed the ceiling. He was a big man; his shoulders were heavily muscled, and muscles rippled down his arms as well. His hands were large and splayed, worn and hardened by work.

"I am a blacksmith," he said. "Would you have use for me in your camp? My family and I do not want to stay longer in the city, although it has been my home since birth."

"By all means," Count Garnier replied. "We would welcome your services. But tell me, what are conditions like in the city, and why do you want to leave it?"

"Yaghi-Siyan has been a good governor, and fair to the Christian community within his walls, up to now. Since their conquest of this city, the Turks have been just rulers, but with your arrival, things have changed. I fear for what is to come, and I would like to help you. The thought of returning Antioch to the fold of God gives me great delight."

"In what way have things changed since our arrival?" Count Garnier asked. "From our vantage point here, nothing has occurred at all."

"From here, perhaps, it looks peaceful and quiet, but within there are stirrings."

"Tell us," the count commanded. "I would know what is going on inside the walls."

"We Christians have been well treated by the governor up to now," Arnulf repeated. His accent was heavy and he searched for words with difficulty. The dialect spoken by the Christians in Antioch was far different from the Frankish tongue. "Our patriarch, John, was permitted to reside with us and tend to our spiritual needs; our churches were allowed to remain Christian and not converted to Muslim. But, since your arrival, Yaghi-Siyan grows angry. The patriarch has been thrown into prison. Many of our leading Christian citizens have been banished, others such as myself have fled. The churches . . ." His voice roughened. "The Cathedral of St. Peter has been desecrated. The emir is using it as a stable for his horses!"

"And the governor," the count asked, "does he seem to be preparing for a long siege?"

"He is, my lord. And is well able to do so. There is abundant water within the walls, market gardens and pasture for any number of flocks. And the troops pass in and out at their pleasure through the western gates to reprovision the city as it needs."

"The mood, then?"

"The mood is one of triumph. The governor is confident he will defeat you."

"I thank you," Count Garnier said. "Theo, see that this man and his family receive food and shelter. I must report to my lord Godfrey on this."

In the days following, more and more Christian refugees slipped out of the city into the encampment. Some, however, came out only to spy, and then slipped back in. By no means were all the Christians within the walls discontented with their lot. Many feared any change. Their life had been peaceful and secure under the Turkish governor. In fact, they paid lower taxes than when the city had been under Byzantine rule. They wanted nothing more than to keep things the way they were and avoid conflict. Some were eager to take any information about the crusaders' plans to the governor, and so curry favor with him.

In this way, Yaghi-Siyan learned of the crusaders' reluctance to attack until reinforcements came, and he began to organize sorties against them. Turkish soldiers crept out from the western gate to cut off any small bands of foraging knights. The governor was clever enough, as well, to plant rumors among the Byzantine Christians that massive Turkish reinforcements were on the way. As the autumn weather turned to winter, and their second Yuletide season found them still so far from Jerusalem, the crusaders' initial optimism died and many began to lose heart.

† † †

"I did not become a man in order to sit and stare at city walls," Emma grumbled as she and Theo sat beside their dying fire one evening.

"You have not become a man at all," Theo answered. His words were short. The wait was hard on him as well. He had celebrated Yuletide in the camp with the priests, but he had not celebrated it in his heart. "And you will have no part in the fighting when it comes," he added.

"That's another thing I want to know about. Why won't you talk about the battles? You have fought now, you've even been wounded. What was it like? Was it glorious?"

"Glorious?" Theo considered the word. "Not glorious. No."

"But to wield a sword! To charge into battle! What could be more spendid?"

"It's what comes after that is not so splendid." Theo paused. "I have killed men, Emma."

"Of course you have. But only your enemies. Only those who would kill you. That is what war is all about, surely."

"You speak more truth than you know. That *is* what war is all about." Theo stirred the embers of the dying fire with the toe of his boot. "I did not know what it would be like when we left Ardennes. My head was full of pomp and glory. We were doing God's bidding . . ."

"And so we are!"

"The first man I killed looked at me as I struck him, Emma, and he knew he was dying. I saw it in his eyes. He was not the enemy then. He was just a man, like me. And there have been so many others—so many."

"I do not understand. I would give anything to be a man and wield a sword for the glory of God." Emma leaped to her feet. "We are fighting God's war, and you—you will be one of the privileged ones to restore Jerusalem to the true faith. How can you speak so gloomily? How can you look so torn?"

In the heat of the moment, she had forgotten all caution. She stood, hood thrown back, face aglow in the light of the fire. A startled voice called out from the edge of their campsite.

"By all that's holy—Emma!"

Emma gave a cry and turned away. She pulled the hood over her head. Too late. Amalric stood across the fire from her, eyes wide with shock.

† † †

"This is madness. Madness." Amalric had repeated the words a dozen times. "You cannot do this, Theo. A servant girl!"

Theo's patience snapped. "She is no mere serving wench. She is kin to Baldwin himself."

"Even worse! Dressed as a man, living with the troops. What if Lord Baldwin finds out? She should be with him, safe under his care. You have lost your wits, Theo."

"She was not safe with him." Theo glared at Amalric. "It is far safer for her to be with me."

"Far more convenient for you, you mean," Amalric said with a sneer, "to have your little wench nearby at night."

Theo reached for his dagger, but Emma forestalled him. So far she had not spoken, but now she put herself between Amalric and Theo, eyes blazing.

"Things are not what you think! Not at all! I cast myself on Theo's mercy because I knew very well what Lord Baldwin's designs on me were. Theo has protected me and cared for me well."

"I'll wager he has."

Emma's hand flashed out. The sound of the slap was echoed by a sudden cracking from a log on the fire. Amalric put a hand to his cheek, eyes wide with astonishment. For a second, there was absolute silence. The three stood frozen. Then Amalric reacted. He raised his own hand and would have struck Emma back if Theo had not leaped forward and grabbed it.

"You would stop me from slapping this insolent slut as she deserves?"

"She is no slut. She is well born and virtuous. You will not touch her."

"The count will hear of this. I promise you that." Amalric wheeled as if to leave.

"Stay!" Theo called out. "Amalric! We are friends—you cannot leave like this!"

"You ask me to overlook this insult?" Amalric was breathing so hard the words came with difficulty.

"I do, for the sake of our friendship. I would not lose that. She will apologize."

"I will not." Emma's voice cut through theirs.

"I do not accept apologies from servants," Amalric growled.

"I do not apologize to those who insult me!"

"Amalric. Emma. We have all lost our tempers. Pray, let us cool down and talk about this." Theo grasped Amalric's arm. "We will drink a little of the wondrous wine they make here, and think about what we must do." His mind was in a fever, trying to find a way out. Emma *will* apologize, he was about to add, but the look on her face silenced him.

"Emma," he said instead. "Please. Fetch us wine. And for yourself as well."

Amalric's eyes followed Emma as she whirled away. They were still hot and angry.

"You are laying up trouble for yourself, my friend."

"Possibly," Theo agreed. "But I knew not what else to do. She appeared at my campsite attired as a groom and determined to accompany me." He had mastered his temper now, and was determined to settle the argument. "I could not send her back to Baldwin, Amalric. Without the lady Godvere there, he would have used her as he wished and then cast her off. I had to protect her."

"She will be discovered. What will you do then?"

"We will be more careful. As long as you say nothing . . ."

Emma returned with skins of wine for Theo and Amalric.

"Join us," Theo said to her.

"No," she replied. She fastened her eyes on Amalric. "I will not apologize," she said. "If I do not defend my own honor, who will? But I will beg of you not to give me away. You were probably within your rights to assume things, but it is not as you think. I serve Theo as his groom, nothing more. And I am a good groom, am I not, Theo?"

Theo managed a nod.

"I beg of you not to give me away," she repeated. The words were humble, but her stance was not. Her eyes were still locked onto Amalric's.

He was the first to look away. He shrugged and laughed.

"I do not make war with maids," he said. "I think you both mad, but I will not interfere. I forgive you." He tossed the last words out as he raised the skin of wine and drank it down.

"I did not ask for forgive—" Emma caught Theo's eye and stopped. "Thank you," she said instead. She turned to go back into her own tent. "And I forgive you," she threw back over her shoulder.

Amalric stiffened. He glared after her. Theo held his breath.

"Truth, that is no ordinary maid," Amalric said finally. His face lightened. "And this is no ordinary wine. Do you have more?"

Twelve

It did not snow in Antioch, but the rains set in just after Christmas. Every day, every night, it poured down incessantly. Every piece of clothing Theo and Emma owned was wet; it was impossible to dry anything. The damp cold seeped into their bones. Emma developed a cough that caused her to double over in pain, gasping for breath, until it was over. Duke Godfrey was seriously ill. His healers were at his bed-side continuously but, despite all their efforts, he seemed not to improve. Bohemond and Raymond sent out a foraging army, but it ran into a Turkish contingent coming to relieve the troops in the city. Weak from hunger and taken by surprise, the crusaders were badly beaten. They suffered enormous losses; the survivors were too weak to continue foraging. Theo and Amalric watched as the remnants of the army straggled back into camp. Emma, hood low over her face, hovered in the background.

"The news?" Theo called to a passing knight.

"Not good," the knight replied. He passed a hand over a forehead caked with dry blood. He was horseless, walking awkwardly with pain or exhaustion, or both.

Amalric strode away without a word.

As Theo, followed closely by Emma, made his way back to his tent, he felt a sudden shifting of the ground under his feet. A curious, rumbling noise began, low at first, then increasing in volume.

"Theo!" Emma cried. The tent in front of them began to sway as if a wind were inside it, then collapsed. Theo reached for a tree to steady himself, but the tree itself was shuddering! He had a moment of complete disorientation. The world was tilting, slipping away from underneath him.

As suddenly as it began, it was over. The rumbling died away, leaving an unnatural silence. For a moment, the camp was completely without sound; not even a bird sang. Then the screaming began. Theo and Emma rushed for their tents. The whole camp was in chaos. Cooking pots had fallen into fires; tents had collapsed, trapping those inside. People were running to and fro in a frenzy, screaming. Miraculously, Theo saw no one who had sustained any injuries. Indeed, there seemed to be more danger to the people in this panic now than there had been during the upheaval.

When Theo and Emma reached their campsite, they found it intact. Centurion grazed imperturbably on the few scrabbly weeds that remained. If the earthquake had bothered him, he showed no signs of it now. Emma's nag side-stepped nervously away from them as they approached, jerking against its tether. It rolled its eyes wildly.

"Stay here, Emma," Theo said. "I must go and see if my foster father is all right."

The count's campsite was adjacent to Theo's. He reached it in a few steps, and was relieved to see that there, too, all seemed in order. Aimery and some of the other men were calming down horses and hysterical servants.

"Theo! Is all well with you?" Aimery called out as he caught sight of him.

"All well, thanks be to God," Theo replied. "Where is my father?"

"He has just left to see the duke and ensure that his camp, also, suffered no harm."

Theo looked around. Aside from one tent that lay in a heap, all was in order. Two of the servants were busy setting it to rights.

"An earthquake, they're calling it. Have you ever seen the like before?" Aimery asked. "Truly, I thought it was the end of the world."

"I've heard of such things," Theo replied, "but never felt one before." He was making an effort to appear calm, but his knees still shook and he had trouble keeping his balance. It was as if his body no longer trusted the stability of the earth.

Around him, the screaming had stopped, and the shouts were gradually dying down. The camp was beginning to return to its normal level of noise and bustle.

But that was not the end of it. That night, as Theo and Emma sat by their campfire, scraping the dregs of a watery stew from their bowls and talking of the incredible thing that had happened, Theo became aware of a crackling intensity in the air. He stopped speaking and looked up, beyond the trees. The rain had ended and the sky was clear.

"Emma," he breathed. "Look!"

Emma raised her head. Above them, the heavens shimmered and shivered with curtains of color. Sheets of green and blue stretched from the horizon to the sky above them. As they watched, the bands dimmed, narrowed, faded to yellow and silver, then blossomed again into vibrant color.

"What does it mean?" Emma asked in a whisper. "First the earth moves, and now this. Is it a portent from God?"

"I know not," Theo answered.

"The earthquake—it was as if God was displeased with us. But this—this is such beauty!"

† † †

The next morning, Theo was awakened by a clamor of voices.

"They can't do this!"

"Sacrilege!"

He thrust his head out of his tent to see men, women and children running toward the edge of the camp nearest the city walls. He pulled on his tunic and ran to join them.

"What's happening?" Emma materialized out of the morning mist beside him.

"Pull down your hood," Theo barked. "Do not speak!" He glanced around quickly to make certain no one had seen or heard her, but the people were too fevered to notice.

"It is the patriarch of Antioch himself!" a woman cried as she rushed by them.

In the general confusion and pandemonium, it was impossible to determine what was happening, but as they reached the walls, the situation became all too clear. Hanging over the wall, suspended in midair, was a cage constructed of rough planks bound together with rope. It swayed in the morning breeze. Inside, a man crouched, clad in a long, brown mantle, clasping

158

a golden cross. As Theo and Emma drew near, they could hear him chanting. One horrified look was enough.

"It *is* the patriarch!" Theo gasped. "How could they inflict this indignity on him! How could they insult God Himself in this manner!"

The patriarch of Antioch, one of the holiest of God's priests—Theo could not believe his eyes. People were dropping to their knees all around; Theo and Emma followed their example.

"God is displeased with us," Bishop Adhemar declared at that morning's mass. "He has set the earth itself to shaking, and the heavens to display His warning. Now He allows the holiest of His servants to be punished for our sins. We are living in sin here. Our soldiers are pillaging and stealing instead of working toward the completion of God's will. There is sloth and laziness instead of planning for the conquering of Antioch and the liberation of Jerusalem. We will fast for three days and pray for His mercy."

Fast they did, but with famine already stalking the campsites, their self-denial made little difference. By February, the crusaders were starving. The countryside all around had been stripped of food, and the peasants' and villagers' winter supplies were exhausted, despite Adhemar's injunctions against thievery. Some began to eat their horses. Sorties from the camp were met with continual ambushes set by the Turks. The loss of knights and troops mounted daily.

"The monk Peter tried to flee," Theo reported to Emma one evening after he had returned from the daily meeting in Godfrey's tent. "Bohemond's brother, Tancred, brought him back."

"Why bother?" Emma answered. "He has been nothing but trouble since he joined us."

"There are many who regard him as a symbol. He was one of the first to follow the pope's call for a crusade."

"And a fine mess he made of it," Emma replied. She was sitting slumped in front of her tent, hood low over her eyes, wiping dust off Centurion's bridle. Her words were low and dispirited.

"We could not have allowed him to leave. It would have caused widespread disillusionment. Too many people are deserting us as it is." But privately, Theo agreed with Emma. The monk raged and disagreed with every decision the crusaders made. He was more of a nuisance than anything else.

† † †

The crusaders could not think of attacking the city until siege engines and mangonels had been constructed, and supplies for those machines had to come from the emperor Alexius. But the bridge of boats was built. Theo and Amalric watched the procedure with amazement. First, the boats themselves were constructed. Flat-bottomed and sturdy, they were lashed together, side by side, from one bank of the river to the other. Then planks were laid across them. When that was completed, a steady, floating bridge spanned the river, strong enough to support knights on horseback.

"Perhaps we have underestimated Taticius and his engineers," Theo remarked to Amalric, as the bridge took shape under their eyes.

As soon as it was completed, the first sortie across was planned.

"It is just what we need," Bohemond told the assembled princes and knights. "A battle to restore our flagging spirits! We will slip out tomorrow before daybreak."

The meeting was being held in Bishop Adhemar's tent. Theo sat at his foster father's side. Godfrey was present as well, but lounged to one side, supported by cushions. He was finally recovering from his illness, but was still weak.

"My scouts tell me that more Turks, under Ridwan of Aleppo, are massing to come to the aid of Antioch," Bohemond said. "They will travel along the road from Aleppo and try to cross the Iron Bridge to the east of us. We will be waiting for them. The infantry will remain in camp to contain any sortie from the city," he continued. "We will take up our position on the other side of the river. Ridwan knows not that we have the means of crossing it now. When he arrives, he will meet a surprise!"

In the darkest hour before dawn, the crusaders snuck out of their camp. Some of the horses balked at stepping onto the floating bridge, but Theo had no trouble with Centurion. The warhorse tested it with one massive forefoot, snuffed at it, then gave his wiry gray mane a shake and moved forward without further hesitation.

The need for absolute silence was paramount. If the Turkish sentries on the walls realized what the crusaders were doing, they would send scouts to warn Ridwan. In front of him and behind him, Theo could hear muffled curses in the black, early morning drizzle. The horses' hooves thudded dully on the wet wood. All metal pieces on bridles and reins had been swathed in cloth to prevent jingling. It was as if an army of ghosts was making its way in the mist across the floating bridge.

Once across, they guided their horses along the northern bank of the river until they reached a hilly outcrop just before the Iron Bridge, out of sight of any Turkish scouts. They took up their position between the river and the Lake of Antioch. In complete silence, they closed up their ranks and waited. It was still the blackest of nights. The cold, unrelenting rain drummed down upon them.

"Why in God's name were we ever cautioned against the sun in Syria?" a voice muttered at Theo's side. He looked over to see Stephen of Blois hunched down into the saddle of his charger. Water streamed down his helmet and made a steady waterfall off the iron nosepiece.

The first traces of dawn began to lighten the sky to the east. Just as the blackness changed to gray, the noise of an approaching army could be heard. Careless and confident, Ridwan's troops made no attempt to be silent.

Trumpets shattered the air. Knights and warhorses were galvanized into action. Theo felt Centurion charge forward before he gave the command. He raised his shield, settled his lance and braced himself for the heavy, bone-shaking lurch of Centurion's gallop. His stomach knotted, but an almost over-whelming joy flooded over him and blotted out everything else. At last, after months of inaction, star-vation and bickering. At last!

The crusaders hit the mass of Turkish soldiers before the advancing army realized what was hap-pening. They gave the Turkish archers no chance to form into lines; they had learned only too well how fearsomely effective the rain of arrows from those archers was. The charge did not break the Turks, however. The trumpets blew for a retreat and the knights withdrew. The Turks, sensing victory, raced after them—and fell straight into a trap that the leaders had cleverly conceived in Adhemar's tent the night before. The crusaders had now lured the Turks onto the very terrain where they wanted them. The lake on the left and the river on the right prevented the great numbers of Turks from surging around the crusaders and outflanking them. With the Turks pressed together in the narrow tract facing them, the crusaders charged.

Theo thrust and thrust again. In the heat of battle, there was no time for thought. It was strike and kill, or be struck and killed. He swung his sword, felt it sink into flesh. At the same time, he felt a blow to his shoulder that almost made him drop his shield. A spray of blood blinded him. He did not know whether it was his adversary's or his own, but in the frenzy of battle he felt no pain. The familiar silence enveloped him. He thrust and cut in a world without noise, a world without screams. He did not even hear the wild, barbaric cries that burst from his own throat.

The Turks broke. They turned and fled.

There was wild celebration in the camp that night. Theo submitted impatiently to Emma's bandaging of his shoulder wound, and then, for the first time, he allowed Amalric to lead him off to the festivities. There, he listened to the boasting and telling of tales of the deeds of the day that grew more and more grand with each horn of wine quaffed. There, the battle as it had really been gradually ascended into the realm of myth and glory; became battle as it was supposed to be. For the first time, the sickness that always attacked Theo after fighting did not overwhelm him. He lost himself in the firelight, the comradeship of fellow warriors, the wine. For the first time, he could forget the feel of his sword sinking into flesh, and the sight of dying eyes staring into his own.

He returned to his tent just before daybreak the next day, befuddled by the wine and the chaos of the celebration. Unseen, in the shadows of the tent where she had been waiting, Emma watched him stagger in.

† † †

With the construction of the bridge, the road to St. Symeon, the Christian port on the sea, was now open to the crusaders. They began to receive supplies sent by ship by the emperor Alexius. A fleet manned by Englishmen and led by Edgar Atheling, the exiled claimant to the English throne, sailed into the port, loaded with siege materials and mechanics sent by the emperor. At last, they could begin to build the machines necessary for the taking of the city.

Hunger was still prevalent, but the famine had been relieved somewhat by the emperor's supplies. Skirmishes between the Turks and the crusaders occurred daily, with great losses on both sides, but gradually the crusaders were able to build towers to guard all the bridges into Antioch. When the final one was completed, the Turks in the city were finally cut off. No convoys of food could reach them now, and the inhabitants could no longer send their flocks to pasture outside the walls. No further sorties could be mounted against the crusaders. The tide began to turn.

Spring came. Almost two years had passed since Godfrey and his crusaders had left their homes in the Ardennes. Theo wondered briefly how his father and brother fared, but he gave them little thought. They seemed part of another, distant world, one that he would probably never see again. His world now was the world of the crusaders. His family was Count Garnier, Amalric and the other men he rode beside every day and stormed into battle with. And Emma. But his feelings about her were so mixed—it was easier just to put them out of his mind. Besides, there was so much else to think about. The rains ceased. Food became plentiful.

"We can do it now," Theo exulted. "We can starve them into submission." There was a hardness in his voice that was new.

Emma stared back at him without answering. Her cough had gone and color was beginning to return to her face, but she was still thin and weak. If she had been quieter and somewhat distant since the night of the battle with Ridwan's army, Theo hadn't noticed.

•Antioch

MEDITERRANEAN SEA

Thirteen

he did, however, notice with a mounting irritation Emma's frequent absences from the campsite. Spring burned into summer. No longer did Stephen of Blois complain about the lack of sun. The June heat was intense, more searing than Theo could have imagined. It bounced and shimmered off the walls. The knights were forced to wear linen coverings over their mail and helmets because the metal became too hot to touch.

As always, the camp was alive with rumors. One was

that the Turk Kerbogha was advancing. But this news was more fact than rumor, Theo believed, as did a great number of crusaders. The stories of Kerbogha's might and cruelty spread throughout the camp, creating panic. He would fall on them from the rear. The garrison would emerge and cut them down from the city. No one would escape. They would all be massacred.

More and more deserters began to slip away during the concealing hours of darkness. The lords and their knights issued commands and posted guards, only to find each morning that the guards had deserted as well. Clearly, the time had come when they must either attack or retreat.

Amalric slipped into Theo's campsite early one morning.

"Bohemond has a plan," he said. He looked around cautiously. "It is a secret; no one must hear of it. Where is Emma?"

"She is not here," Theo answered. He cast an annoyed glance at Centurion, who had not yet been groomed. Where was Emma, anyway?

As if to echo his irritation, Centurion blasted out a snort that sent Emma's nag skittering.

Theo thrust Emma out of his mind. "What kind of plan?"

"There is a man," Amalric said, his voice low. "He is an Armenian, a Christian now converted to Islam. He is a captain inside the city. His name is Firouz. He has a high position in Yaghi-Siyan's government, or so he claims. He has been loyal so far, but now he is angry. His master fined him for hoarding grain, and he is beginning to regret his conversion. He wishes to come back to the true faith. He has got in touch with Bohemond through a Christian in our camp—Arnulf, a blacksmith."

Theo looked up, surprised.

"What?" Amalric asked.

"Nothing," Theo answered. "I know the man, that is all. He is to be trusted, I think. Go on."

"Well," Amalric continued, "Firouz will sell the city to us. To Bohemond, anyway. I have some suspicions about this need for secrecy. It smells to me as if Bohemond is plotting to be in command when the fighting is all over."

"I have no doubt of it," Theo answered. "And I could not care less. Someone will have to govern."

"Why should it be Bohemond? My lord is equally fit to govern."

"Bohemond and the other lords have never stopped arguing about who is in command of this crusade since we left Constantinople. I, for one, am sick of the squabbling. What does it matter?" Theo jumped to his feet and strode over to Centurion. He began to groom the horse with quick, angry strokes. When Centurion turned his great head and glowered at him, Theo moderated his touch.

"It matters—" Amalric began, but at that moment Emma appeared.

Startled, she stopped and pulled her hood farther down over her face, then relaxed as she recognized Amalric. The two of them had come to a truce that was beginning to develop into actual friendship. She would have greeted him, but Theo interrupted.

"Where have you been? Centurion has not been groomed. The morning fire has not been kindled."

Emma shrugged. "I had business of my own."

"You are my groom. Your only business is my business," Theo snapped back. In the morning light, he saw a flush rise to her cheeks. "I'm sorry," he said. "I spoke hastily. I meant not . . ."

"You are quite right," Emma replied. Her voice was cold. "I must not forget that I am the servant of such a great warrior." She bent to the fire and made a show of arranging sticks and kindling.

Amalric looked from one to the other and raised his eyebrows. "A lovers' spat?" He laughed.

Both Theo and Emma whipped around to glare at him.

"Mercy! It was said in jest. I give you my apologies!" He turned to go, then half turned back. "Come to Godfrey's tent this evening, Theo. There will be news by then, I am certain of it."

† † †

They did not have to wait that long. Shortly after the noon meal and prayers, a herald galloped around the camp, trumpet blaring. They were to prepare for a raid into enemy territory at sunset. Even as Theo and Emma began organizing his equipment, Theo puzzled over the summons. Why a raid just now, when they should be preparing to attack the city itself?

"It may be a bluff," Emma said, polishing Centurion's bridle and testing a suspected weak spot in the leather.

She seemed to be right. Or perhaps the secret had not been kept as well as Bohemond had wished. Secret or not, the news had probably traveled, as news was wont to do, throughout the web of servants and grooms. Somehow Emma had learned how to tap into that web, despite her pretended muteness.

Another messenger followed more quietly, bidding the nobles and their knights to assemble in Bohemond's tent.

"Firouz is in command of one of the wall towers—the Tower of the Two Sisters, they call it," Bohemond announced when they had all gathered. "He is ready to betray the city. He urges us to mount our attack on the walls at that spot. He will give over the tower to us, and then we can seize the others."

Theo's blood began to beat more loudly in his ears and he felt the now familiar excitement rising within him. His fingers opened and closed on the hilt of his sword as Bohemond outlined the plan for the next day. The urge to withdraw the weapon was almost overpowering.

At sunset, with great fanfare and amid a cacophony of preparations, the army set out eastward as if to intercept Kerbogha. Theo mounted Centurion and gathered up the bridle.

"Go with God," Emma said. She gave Centurion a last stroke on his broad, stone-hard forehead, then stepped back.

"Thank you," Theo said. He reached to grasp her shoulder, but she had already moved away; his hand closed on empty air. He hesitated a moment, then urged Centurion on. There was something about Emma—something strange in her manner. He turned back one last time before he was out of sight of the campfire, but she was no longer there. He stared at the empty site. It was odd that she had not waited until he had ridden out of sight. Odd...

"Theo! Make haste!" Amalric's voice rang out over the general noise and confusion.

Theo set spurs to Centurion and fell in beside him.

† † †

The cavalry led, as usual; the infantry and the archers toiled over the hill paths behind it. Bohemond kept the pace slow so the different parts of the army would not be separated. They marched until night was well upon them; only then did the trumpets signal a halt. As the vast army came to a stop, orders were shouted down along the ranks, from the knights to the infantry and the archers. The army turned and began to march back, this time in silence. Bridles and reins were muffled; no man spoke.

Just before dawn, Theo saw the Tower of the Two Sisters loom up out of the darkness before them. All was quiet. There was no sign of a guard. The vast army materialized out of the surrounding hills almost without a sound.

A small detachment of about sixty knights, led by Bohemond, dismounted and crept forward. Theo was annoyed to find that Emma was not there, as they had agreed, to take Centurion, so he left the horse instead with Amalric's groom. He was puzzled at her failure to appear, but there was no time to dwell on it because Count Garnier was signaling to him. The count and Duke Godfrey were at Bohemond's side. Amalric and Theo followed closely. Some of the knights carried a long, wooden ladder. Still in the utmost silence, they placed it against the tower. One by one, the knights climbed up it and through a window high on the wall. Theo found himself behind Amalric. The ladder shook under the weight of the knights climbing above him. The rungs felt rough under his leather-shod feet. He climbed awkwardly, his chain mail heavy and impeding.

Amalric disappeared through the opening. Theo held his breath, waiting for an outcry, but the night was still. He reached for the last rung, then grasped the stone sill. With one mighty effort, he heaved himself over and inside. His linen shift muffled the jingling of his mail somewhat, but the slight noise still sounded loud to his ears. He struggled to his feet. Around him in the pitch dark he could sense, more than see, the assembled knights.

"This way," a voice hissed. Theo turned toward it and saw a figure silhouetted by torchlight in the open doorway. This must be the Armenian, Firouz, Theo thought. Following his silent directions, the knights slipped out of the room and made their way, some to the left and some to the right, to the other two towers that were under Firouz's control. Then they signaled to the rest of the waiting army below. Ladders were raised; the army poured up them.

At this, Bohemond gave the order to attack. The walls and battlements suddenly rang with the clash of weapons, and shouts shattered the dark stillness of the night. Theo drew his sword and rushed forward, Amalric at his side. Men tried to block them but together, shields protecting each other, they cut the Turks down and stormed along the wall and into the city. Their first objective was to open the city gates to the rest of the crusading army. To Theo's surprise, a horde of people surged to their aid: the Christians of Antioch were roused and ready to fight. Within minutes, the two main gates of the city were opened, and the mass of infantrymen and archers poured through.

Under this onslaught, the Turks were soon in full rout. Yaghi-Siyan and his bodyguard fled from the city and up the gorge that led to the Iron Gate. No one bothered to pursue him. His son, Shams ad-Daula, did not follow him, but instead led his followers up to the citadel at the mountain peak.

"After them!" The cry went up. Theo and Amalric, behind Bohemond, raced to follow, but were checked at the entrance. The citadel was solid stone and well fortified. Once inside, the Turks were safe. Frustrated, Bohemond nonetheless planted his purple banner on the highest point he could reach.

"We cannot get in, but they cannot get out. Let them stay in there like the trapped rats they are!" Amalric shouted. As the sun rose and touched Bohemond's banner with glints of gold, a great cheer arose from the crusaders. The knights turned and forged their way back down into the city.

The fight was over; the looting and sacking began. At first, the morning echoed and re-echoed with screams, but by nightfall they had ceased. Not a Turk was left alive in Antioch. The head of Yaghi-Siyan was brought to Bohemond by a peasant and impaled beside the purple banner so that his son might look out upon it from his refuge in the citadel. The houses of the citizens of Antioch were pillaged. In the chaos, not even the houses of the Christians were spared. Treasures were scattered or wantonly destroyed. Corpses lay in the streets, already beginning to rot in the summer heat.

Count Garnier and his men were assigned houses in the center of the city. Theo helped to clear them of bodies. The corpses were piled in the streets to be burned. It was late at night by the time the job was done.

"Go, Theo, rest. You deserve it. You have fought well today," his foster father told him finally. Theo was too exhausted to argue. He retrieved Centurion from Amalric's groom, then stumbled to the house the count had designated his. Of Emma, there was not a trace.

The house he had been given was built of white stone, and had a garden that someone had tended lovingly. The heavy scent of many flowers filled the air and mingled with the stench of blood and bodies. Theo unsaddled Centurion, found water for him, and tethered him to graze. He sank down on the front steps of the house. His mind teemed with the memory of streets filled with bodies, and of soldiers running amok and slicing down every person they saw. He had not taken part in that madness, but he had not been able to stop it, either. He dropped his head into his hands and retched. This sickness was worse, far worse, than any he had ever suffered before. It was not just a sickness of the body. It was a sickness of his very soul.

A commotion at the gate startled him.

"Your boy! It seems he decided to become a fighting man." It was Guy. A body was slung over his shoulder. "A womanly chap like this—you should whip some sense into him. I told you, did I not, that you spoil him?"

Theo leaped to his feet. Guy dumped the body on the ground.

"We are even now. A favor for a favor. A life for a life." Incredibly, he smiled. His face was covered in blood. His eyes glittered in the torchlight from the street. "Although I warrant this life is of very little value. Nevertheless, I pay my debts." He turned and left.

Theo stared down at the body. Blood had seeped into the heavy, woollen tunic of the boy lying there. His short hair was matted and covered his face. An empty archer's quiver was slung across his back; his left hand still clutched a bow.

It wasn't possible. Theo's eyes refused to see what lay before him. Only when the body moved and a moan escaped the bloodless lips did he allow himself to recognize Emma.

Antioch

MEDITERRANEAN SEA

Fourteen

Theo knelt to examine her. In the dim, smoldering light, it was impossible to tell how badly she was injured. He ran out into the street and wrested one of the torches from the ground, then set it into the earth beside her. He knelt again. Blood had soaked into her tunic around the left shoulder. He pulled his knife from his belt and cut the tunic away. An ugly gash ran from the bone under her neck halfway to the shoulder. It did not seem too deep, and was no longer bleeding, but Theo knew she must have lost a lot of blood already. He picked her up and made his way into the house with her, shocked at how light her body felt in his arms.

In the unfamiliar darkness inside the house, he tripped and then realized he had stumbled into a low bed of some kind. He laid Emma down on it and went back outside for the torch. By its light, he managed to locate a dish of oil with a wick floating in it, and made a light. He leaned over Emma again. Her hand still gripped the bow. He loosened her fingers and took the weapon from her, then slipped the quiver off her back so she could lie more comfortably. Now, he had to clean the wound. He had found a well in the yard when he had tended to Centurion. He could get water there.

He was trying to think calmly, to do the things that had to be done, one at a time. He was trying not to think beyond that—not to think that Emma might be dying. He *wouldn't* think that. He straightened and went out to the well. An earthen bowl lay on the ground where it had probably been dropped that morning by whoever lived here. Used to live here . . . He filled it with water and went back to Emma.

She had not moved. Nor had she made a sound since that single moan.

Theo tore a strip of cloth from the bed covering, wet it and began to bathe the gash. When he was finished, he tore more strips and bound the wound as tightly as he could. He fought down the urge to run and try to find one of the healers that accompanied the crusaders. He dared not leave Emma for so long. If she awoke, alone and confused, there was no telling what she might do. The flow of blood was stanched; all he could do now was wait.

He sank down onto the floor beside the low bed and drew his knees up to his chest. He wrapped his arms around them, but kept his head upright, eyes fixed on Emma.

Whatever had possessed her? How had she managed to take part in the battle? The bow, the quiver— who had taught her archery? He began to think back to all her unexplained absences. Finally, he could not stave off the thought any longer: what if she died? No Emma? In an instant, the future turned bleak.

Toward morning, he slept. He was awakened by the first rays of the sun striking in through a window. The wick had burned out. Heat already hung heavy around him, and the smell from the streets outside permeated the room. Today would be spent disposing of bodies before they rotted even more. He couldn't face the thought.

"Theo?"

Emma's eyes were open and fixed upon him. Her face was flushed and covered in sweat. Theo dipped a clean rag in the bowl of water and knelt beside her to bathe her forehead.

"Where are we, Theo? How did I come here? I remember a sword . . . a sword flashing down upon me. I thought I would die. What happened?"

"Guy saved you. He found you lying wounded and brought you here."

"Guy? I thought he hated you. I know he disliked me. Why would he help me?"

"God alone knows. He is a strange person."

"Did he realize . . . that I am not . . ."

"No. By the grace of God, he did not."

"Just as well I am so scrawny." She attempted a smile and tried to raise her head, then dropped it back. "Where are we?"

"In a house. It has been given to me."

"Given to you? By whom? Whose house is it?"

These were questions Theo did not want to answer. He evaded them by going for clean water. When he came back, he knelt beside her once more.

"Why did you do this, Emma?" he asked.

"I wanted to fight, to be a part of it." She turned her head away, but not before Theo saw her eyes fill with tears.

He reached to bathe her forehead again.

"Rest then, Emma," he said. "We will talk later. I'm going to make a soup now—you need nourishment. Then I'll find a healer to tend to you."

"No!"

"Why not? You need a healer. Your wound is grave, it must be seen to."

"No!" She made a feverish effort to rise, then let out a cry of pain and sank back onto the bed. "You must not bring a healer, Theo. He will see that I am not a boy. I will be discovered!"

"But, Emma, you might die!"

"I will not die." Weak as she was, she dashed the tears away and managed to glare at him. "I'm not ready to die. Make me some soup and cleanse my wound and we'll see this through together—just you and I."

"You *must* see a healer."

"I will not. If you bring one to me, I will scream and carry on so much that it will probably do me even more harm."

Theo looked at her. Her face was set in a way he knew only too well.

"Soup, Theo. That's what I need. I pray you, good, hot broth. I will not die, I promise you."

Nor did she. Theo nursed her every moment he could steal away from his duties to the count, and gradually she began to mend.

"Truly, that maid has a will of iron," Amalric said one evening a fortnight later. He had come to share the evening meal with Theo, and Emma had insisted on sitting up with them. He looked at her and shook his head. "I would not have you for an enemy, Emma."

"And why should you?" Emma retorted. "As long as you keep my secret, we should be the best of friends."

"The best of friends," Amalric repeated. "The best of friends with a groom, who is really a nursemaid, who is really kin to a nobleman, and who decided to become an archer and go to war. An odd turn to my life, indeed."

Emma raised an eyebrow. "An adjustment that a clever young knight such as yourself can make, I vow."

"Emma . . ." Theo began warningly. Why did she always go too far? Why could she not at least pretend to maidenly modesty?

"I tire," Emma said. "I would sleep now. I'll leave you two to settle the affairs of the land by yourselves."

"A mercy," Amalric replied.

✝   ✝   ✝

When the triumphant celebrations attending their victory died down, the crusaders took stock. They were inside Antioch now, and had the walls and towers of the city to protect them from Kerbogha when he attacked. All their civilian followers were sheltered as well within the walls, and were no longer the liability they had been outside. They could now be defended with ease. But there were problems.

"We do not have enough men to defend all the walls," Duke Godfrey said. "The walls are too long. And we must build another barrier between us and the citadel, or we will be attacked from there one night. Shams ad-Daula is in an enviable position to keep watch on us and report all of our movements to Kerbogha, while we can do nothing about it."

"Can we not mount another attack on the citadel?" Amalric strode back and forth in front of his foster father. "Surely, we must not just let Shams ad-Daula abide there."

"There is nothing else we can do for the moment," the duke replied. "Lord Bohemond has said that we must begin readying ourselves for the arrival of Kerbogha. We must find provisions, too. The city was much more in need than I had realized. There are practically no stores of food left." He did not add that the crusaders themselves, in their madness, had destroyed most of the city's wealth.

Little by little, order was restored. The patriarch John was released from prison and put back on the patriarchal throne. The Bishop of Le Puy had the Cathedral of St. Peter and the other desecrated churches cleaned and restored to Christian worship.

Early one morning, Theo awoke to a stirring in the city. He dressed quickly and sought out his foster father.

"Kerbogha and his army have arrived," the count said. He led Theo to one of the wall towers. Looking out from between the battlements, Theo could see the Turkish army encamped in the very positions the crusaders had occupied. He stared in awe at the sheer number of men. Tents stretched out along the walls for as far as he could see in either direction. The encampment teemed with soldiers, archers and horses—a moving, seething mass of brilliant color. The noise was indescribable. Men shouted, horses neighed and whinnied. Dozens of camels added their outlandish brays to the din.

Before the week was out, Kerbogha had reinforced the citadel above his troops and encircled the city completely. Cut off from any hope of foraging or replenishing their supplies, the crusaders were now the besieged, and the Turks the besiegers.

"Only the emperor can help us now," Theo said to Emma. "He must send troops to help us."

Emma was grooming Centurion. Her own nag had been lost or stolen during the battle. She came every day to Theo's house to perform her duties for him, but she refused to live there, preferring instead to pitch her tent in a nearby field.

"There are bloodstains on the floors," she said when Theo offered her one of the rooms. "Bloodstains from innocent people—a family, perhaps. I could not possibly live here."

Theo tried to persuade her, but his arguments were weak. In truth, he himself felt uncomfortable in the house and spent as little time there as possible. The knowledge that its former owners had undoubtedly been killed in the slaughter was just one more thing he did not wish to think about.

Emma paused to take a rest. She was still weak, but insisted on carrying out her groom's duties in spite of any protests Theo might make.

"If we are to depend on the emperor, then we are finished for certain," she said.

Theo shook his head. "We must have faith. We are here at his bidding, after all, to help regain Jerusalem and his lost empire."

"To fight his battles for him and reconquer the cities his Byzantine Empire has lost—that I am certain he desires us to do. But I doubt he wishes to help us much to do it—not if he has to put his own men in peril. And as for our quest to liberate Jerusalem, that is of no consequence to him whatsoever, I fear."

That evening, news came that Stephen of Blois and a company of other noblemen and knights had slipped out of Antioch and were on their way to the port of St. Symeon.

"Deserting rats," Emma said.

"Not so," Theo argued. "They will tell the emperor of our plight. They will make him send help."

"You are innocent as a babe, Theo. They will save their own skins, that is all."

Rumor was quick to prove her right.

"The traitor!" Amalric burst into his friend's house the next night as Theo was preparing for sleep.

"Who? What has happened?"

"Stephen of Blois. A scout just came back. The emperor did send the imperial army. The men were on their way to help us, but they met Stephen and he told them we were lost. He told them there was no hope for us. The army turned back!"

"And the emperor believed him?" Theo asked.

"Why should he not?" Amalric answered.

"Why should he not, indeed." Emma's voice came out of the shadows of the garden. "It gives him reason for abandoning us—for not risking the lives of his soldiers."

"So, this is how the Greeks repay us," Theo said.

"This is how," Amalric replied.

†   †   †

Two days later, Kerbogha attacked. Before the crusaders could mount an effective defense, his soldiers took possession of one of the towers on the southwestern wall. Bohemond responded by ordering the whole section of the city around that tower to be burned. Streets, houses, all went up in flames. When the fires died down, troops of halberdiers and archers were sent to fill the area and mount guard against the Turkish troops in the tower.

"And the people who were living there—what of them?" Emma asked.

"They will have to find other dwellings," Amalric answered.

"How grateful these Christians must be to us for liberating them from the Turks," Emma said.

"It is war," Amalric answered shortly. "These things cannot be helped."

"I am beginning to understand more and more what this thing called war really is," Emma said. "Not at all what they had us believe when we first started out on this venture, is it?"

Theo looked away from her. Amalric was right. Of course, he was. How could Emma be expected to understand?

Fifteen

"We are starving. No help is forthcoming. We must fight."

Bohemond drew up the battle plans with all the leaders in a tent that was ominously quiet. There were no arguments, no suggestions. Theo and Amalric stood by the door and listened.

"We are vastly outnumbered," Bohemond said, "but we will make the best use of what we have. I will divide our troops into six armies. Two hundred men will be left in the city to keep watch on the citadel."

Theo and Amalric exchanged a tense look, but their worry was short-lived. They were to be among the attacking force.

"You will not sneak out with the army this time, Emma," Theo said when he returned to his house. He was about to say, "I forbid it," but stopped himself in time. Those words might be all she needed to decide to go. To his surprise, she gave him no argument.

"I have had my war," she answered. "I begin to think war is men's work after all. I want nothing further to do with it."

"It is God's work," Theo replied. "How else could we liberate His holy city?"

"God's work? Killing innocent people? Torching their homes and destroying everything they own? You yourself tried to tell me what it was like. *You* were shocked by the killing. I didn't understand then, but I have learned. I, too, saw men killed." Her voice faltered. "I, too, have killed."

"You can't be certain of that. An archer never knows where his arrows go in the fury of battle. It is not the same as striking a man down with a sword."

"I *am* certain. I saw the man fall, pierced by an arrow from my bow. It was at that moment, when I stood frozen, realizing what I had done, that I was struck down. The feeling is the same, Theo. Killing is killing."

"Killing is necessary." The words came out of Theo's mouth in a harsh voice that didn't sound like his. He rubbed a hand over his eyes. He was suddenly tired. He did not want to debate this with Emma. His duty was clear: he would follow his foster father and their leaders to war, to do God's work.

"Even the bishop himself makes war, Emma. Tomorrow, many of the priests will march into battle with us. Surely, they understand God's will. It is not for us to question."

"But I do," Emma replied. She turned away. "Anyway, you need not fear for me in the battle tomorrow. I will not be there."

† † †

Theo rode out with the knights at dawn. Each contingent was under its own banner, but he could not help seeing that the banners were tarnished, the panoply of war no longer as glistening and glorious as it had been. There was a worn and weary air to the men who marched and rode with him. Many knights were horseless. They marched on foot or rode donkeys and mules. Theo felt a sense of desperation in the air. This was a battle they *had* to win.

They filed out through the gates and over the fortified bridge that protected the city. Massed on the horizon, frozen in silence, Kerbogha's mighty army waited.

"Look!" Amalric hissed. He was riding behind Godfrey at Theo's side, as usual.

A herald detached himself from the Turkish army and rode across the field toward them. Theo waited for Bohemond to give the signal to pause. The signal was not given. Instead, the crusaders spread out into their appointed positions as soon as they had made the crossing. There were to be no negotiations.

The herald wheeled his horse around and galloped back to the Turkish ranks. As if nervous at this show of confidence by the crusaders, Kerbogha's army fell back.

A great shout arose from the crusaders and they surged forward. Trumpets blared, but if the command to halt was given, the eager knights heeded it not. Fooled by the very same trick they had used with the Turks, they galloped across the level field chosen by Bohemond as a good fighting ground, and were lured into the hills. Several of the horses stumbled in the rougher terrain. A few went down, carrying their riders, cursing, with them.

"It is a trap!" Theo shouted, as Kerbogha wheeled his army back to face the crusaders, archers at the ready. A hail of arrows shot into the crusaders' ranks. Theo felt one whistle by his cheek. More horses went down, their screams mingling with the cries of the surprised knights. A section of Kerbogha's army detached itself from the main body and galloped to outflank the crusaders on their left.

"Stop them!" Bohemond cried. Theo and Amalric charged, side by side.

Theo saw Bishop Adhemar's standard-bearer fall. The flag was instantly trampled into shreds, but the bishop himself was fighting still. Theo's sword flashed in the morning sunlight. Over and over it rose and fell, rose and fell. Theo lost count of the number of men he struck. The familiar, wild lust took over. The familiar, welcome silence descended upon him, wrapping him in a cocoon of invulnerability.

Only gradually did he realize the Turks were falling back. He was shocked to discover they were retreating. Beside him, Amalric let out a whoop of victory and spurred his warhorse on. Centurion, half-crazed, surged after him. Together with their comrades, they chased the fleeing army as far as the Iron Bridge, killing all they caught up to. Some of the Turks sought shelter in the keep that Tancred had constructed near the bridge. Theo only had time to see a group of crusaders surround them before he hurtled past. Their screams followed him, and then were lost behind him.

Finally, the fields before them were empty. There was no one left to kill. The crusaders reined in their warhorses and turned back, triumphant, to the city. At the gates, Bohemond turned to face his army.

"Send a message to the emperor!" he cried. "Antioch is ours!"

"Our victory is complete," Godfrey announced with satisfaction when he had gathered his knights together the following day. "The Syrians and the Armenians in the surrounding countryside have finished our work for us. Reports tell me they have killed all the remnants of Kerbogha's army they could find, and the citadel has surrendered to us."

"Now, to celebrate," Amalric gloated.

"Our leaders are quarreling already over who is to command the city," Theo said.

"What matters that to us?" Amalric responded.

† † †

"There is much sickness in the camp," Emma reported as she groomed Centurion a few days later.

"There is always sickness," Theo answered.

"Not like this. I fear it is a plague, Theo."

Theo felt a stab of fear, quickly followed by a rising anger. Were they never to be spared?

"Bishop Adhemar is sick."

The priests offered prayers daily for his recovery, but to no avail. The whole crusading army was stunned when they finally announced his death. The bishop had been a true hero of the crusade, one of the few people whom everyone followed and trusted.

The summer heat mounted; more and more victims succumbed to sickness. Aimery, Count Garnier's beloved squire, took sick when the plague was at its height. The count himself nursed him, but he died. Theo mourned with his foster father. Aimery had been Theo's friend from childhood. To

Theo, it seemed as if the last vestige of his boyhood was now gone.

Most of the crusaders thought the plague was carried in the air and that nothing could be done to avoid it, but Emma believed otherwise. She was convinced the disease lay in dirt, and she scrubbed Theo's house with a determined fury every day. She boiled all their woollen clothes over the fire until they were shrunken and stiff, and Theo forbade her to touch another of his garments. Then, from somewhere, she procured tunics and shifts of linen for them that were far cooler to wear, and could be washed as often as she pleased.

"All this washing and cleaning is not groom's work, Emma," Theo remonstrated. "People will think you odd."

"They already think so." Emma shrugged. "That is of no importance."

Thanks either to her industry or plain good fortune, Theo and Emma survived. Amalric also made it through the epidemic unscathed—and without Emma's obsessive cleanliness, he was quick to point out.

"The devil takes care of his own, they say," Emma replied with a sniff.

But the nobles still delayed their departure to Jerusalem. Summer ended and the cooler winds of winter began to blow.

"Our leaders fight constantly among themselves," Theo told Emma bitterly. "The emperor has sent word that now, after we have secured the city without any help from him, *now* he will come to Antioch. And our princes will not budge until he arrives."

"Why do they so wish to see him?" Emma asked. "I thought the only thing they could agree on was their hatred of him."

"Oh, they hate him well enough," Theo replied. "But he will undoubtedly bring rich gifts and rewards, and none of them wish to be done out of their share of that."

"Have you heard?" Amalric asked one morning as he joined Theo and the count for their first meal. "Jerusalem has been taken from the Turks by the Egyptians—the Fatimids!"

"What does this mean?" Theo asked.

"Nothing to us, as far as Bohemond is concerned," Amalric answered. "The Fatimids are Muslims, the same as the Turks they conquered. We will simply fight them instead of the Turks when we get there."

"*If* we get there," Theo muttered. "Our leaders would rather sit here and rot than get on with it."

"We will go soon, my son," the count assured him. "I have heard that the soldiers and the common folk have had enough of all this haggling, and I, for one, agree with them. They have threatened to march on their own and tear down the walls of Antioch as they leave if we do not come to some decision."

Amalric frowned. He would tolerate no talk that even remotely sounded like criticism of Duke

Godfrey, but he could not argue with Count Garnier.

"Three Yuletides, now, since we left our homes," Emma said, when Count Garnier had left and she had joined Theo and Amalric. She was always careful to stay far away when the count was present. "Who would have thought the journey would take so long?"

"Much has happened," Theo said. He scraped the last of the gruel from his bowl.

"Much," Emma agreed. She rubbed her finger around the rim of her bowl and then licked it. "We were so young when we left, were we not?"

Theo looked at her in surprise. In the privacy of the house, with only Amalric there, she had thrown back her hood, and Theo saw her clearly for the first time in months. There were lines around her eyes. Her mouth had a firmness and determination that had not been there before. In truth, she was a young, carefree girl no more. He supposed that he, too, had changed just as much.

"Well, I, for one, am still young, and I intend to remain so for the rest of my life. I will never grow old," Amalric announced.

"How will you accomplish that, my friend?" Theo asked.

"Live well, die young. In battle, preferably. That is the life I choose."

Theo searched his friend's face carefully. Amalric had not changed very much. His eyes were still bright and eager, his brow was unlined. There was, perhaps, a hardness that had not been there before, but that was all.

"The warrior's life suits you," Theo said.

"It does," Amalric agreed. "Most admirably."

It was true, Theo thought. Amalric fought when he had to fight, and enjoyed life to the hilt whenever he could. He was plagued by none of the doubts, the fears, the waves of sick desperation that overwhelmed Theo.

† † †

Finally, in January, they left. The weather was pleasantly cool as they made their way through the hills south of the city toward the coast. Theo's palfrey had died in the summer heat at Antioch, so he often walked with Emma, leading Centurion. He had a small Turkish pony that had been captured during the battle, but used it to carry their possessions, as he did not want to load Centurion even lightly. The long journey was taking its toll on the warhorse. He had been able to rest in Antioch most of the time, but now he was forced to cover many kilometers each day. Theo worried about him. He had not been bred to do this kind of work. The horse sweated profusely and some evenings refused to graze, just stood, head hanging with exhaustion and dejection. Emma tempted him with the sweetest grass and leaves she could find but, more often than not, he rejected them.

It was only when they had crossed the mountains and began to near the sea that he seemed to revive.

Theo could feel a difference in the air now. There was a salty tang to the breezes that sprang up in the early mornings. Tales began to be told among the crusaders of the immensity of the sea toward which they traveled.

"It stretches to the very end of the world," Amalric reported with authority.

In the end, however, nothing could have prepared Theo for the sight of it when they finally reached its rocky shores. An endless, moving, shining expanse. The waves murmured in, one after another. Wet, shiny seaweed festooned the rocks. When he bent to touch it, the water was warm, welcoming.

The first evening, after camp had been set up, Emma and Theo stole away to a secluded cove near their campsite. Out of sight of any of the other crusaders, Emma shed, for a few moments, her groom's disguise. She dropped onto a rock, tore off her worn, stiff leather shoes, and dangled her bare feet in the water with a sigh of absolute bliss. Theo could not bring himself to enjoy quite such a liberty, but he sank down beside her. At first, afraid someone would come upon them, he sat tense and alert, but gradually the quietness and beauty of the evening soothed and settled him.

They didn't speak. A few seabirds swooped out over the waves. Their cries sounded strangely mournful and lost. Behind them, the noise and bustle of the army and the pilgrims making camp were muted, as if they came from another world.

Suddenly, Emma stood and waded out into the softly plashing surf. Theo watched as she bent to run her fingers lightly through the water, as if caressing the small waves. She straightened up again, and then ventured a few steps farther out. A wave, larger than the others, caught her by surprise. She staggered with the force of it, then found her balance and turned back to face Theo, laughing.

"Come in, Theo," she cried. "Join me!"

He shook his head.

"But it's wonderful!"

When he still did not move to follow her, she made a face at him, shrugged her shoulders and splashed back to sit beside him. Her toes curled around the rocks. He felt the warmth of her body against him, smelled the musky, earthy smell of her . . . He stiffened and forced himself to draw away.

Emma had made it very clear what their bargain was.

Sixteen

"An envoy arrived last evening from the Fatimid Eyptians," Amalric announced one morning.

It was early April and the army had halted once again after traveling south, following the shores of the great sea. The heat increased daily, but there were always sea breezes to offset it, and the country-side was green and fertile. Orchards were in blossom. Beyond them, farther inland, snow-topped crests of mountains gleamed in the sun.

The crusaders were quarreling again. Raymond of

Toulouse had led his troops inland to lay siege to the town of Arga. Even though the town was of little importance to the crusade and the other princes refused to support him, he would not desist. Word had come from the emperor Alexius that he would join them by June, and once again Raymond intended to wait for him.

"We are nearing the Fatimids' territory, are we not?" Emma looked up from where she was trimming the long hair around Centurion's hooves. It collected mud and dirt and made the going harder for him. When she didn't immediately resume the work, the horse gave her a nudge that knocked her back on her heels. She righted herself and gave him a good-natured cuff on the ear. The warhorse was suffering now with the heat as well, and she was inclined to humor him.

Not that she ever did otherwise, Theo thought.

"We are," Amalric answered. "The Fatimids have driven the Turks out as far as the Dog River, a scant week's travel from here."

"And what did the messenger have to say?" Theo asked.

"He brought an offer from the Egyptian vizier, al-Adfal. He promised that if we abandon any attempt to force our way into their territory, they will allow us free access to all the holy places in Jerusalem."

"And Bohemond's answer?"

"He rejected it. Jerusalem must be Christian again—nothing less will do. The envoy went away furious. He said we will all be killed like dogs."

They celebrated Easter amid palm trees that Christ Himself must have looked upon. A month later, the count told Theo that the princes had convinced Raymond to abandon his siege of Arga.

"The fighting has cost the lives of many of his men," he told Theo, his voice weighted with sadness.

When the remainder of Raymond's men rode, sagging and defeated, back into the crusader camp, Theo saw rivulets of tears staining channels down Raymond's dirt-encrusted cheeks.

"Not a prince who accepts failure easily," Amalric muttered.

† † †

"Finally, we move again," Theo announced to Emma early the next day. They struck camp and the army continued its progress down the coast, through the small seaport of Jabala, where the emir surrendered to them with hardly any resistance, and on to the port of Tortosa, where the inhabitants made no resistance at all.

"I see that our army is behaving with its usual gratitude and respect for those who do not oppose us," Emma remarked, as she stood by Theo and watched soldiers march into camp with animals that they had captured on raids into the surrounding countryside. Ponies, goats and even more of the curious camels were led in. The camels could go for the most amazing periods of time without water, but they were not suited for riding, Theo discovered. He had tried it, and found that the rolling lurch of the beast made Centurion seem a model of comfort and ease in comparison.

They reached Tripoli, where the emir greeted them effusively.

"He has not only released three hundred Christians that he has been holding captive, but he's given them fifteen thousand bezants in compensation and fifteen fine horses," Amalric reported. "He's provided us with pack animals and provender for the entire army as well."

"Only too glad to see us on our way out of his city and supplied well enough to tackle the Fatimids for him," Emma remarked.

"She is probably right," Amalric admitted. "The Egyptians press ever closer. It will make the emir feel much better to have us as a buffer between him and them."

The army warily approached the Fatimid frontier at the Dog River. Although shallow here, the river was a fast-flowing stream that cut its way down through boulders and rocks from the wooded mountains above to hurl itself into the sea. Both Theo and Emma rode Turkish ponies now, and carried their supplies on one of the emir's pack animals. Centurion plodded beside them, head down and sweating profusely. He waded into the cool water and stood there, letting the current swirl around and past him as if he were one of the great boulders themselves.

"Move him out of there," Theo ordered Emma. "He is in the way."

"He will not move," Emma replied.

"Make him," Theo insisted.

"I cannot," she said.

"You cannot?" Theo echoed. He scowled.

"No," Emma answered, "I cannot. He will move when he wishes."

Theo's scowl deepened. "You spoil that animal entirely too much," he said. "I will not have this." He strode into the water and took hold of Centurion's reins.

Emma relinquished them and made her way to the river's edge. There she stood, hands behind her back, and watched. Her hood covered most of her face, but Theo could see a small smile twitching at the corners of her mouth. He tugged on Centurion's bridle. It was like tugging on a stone wall. He tugged again. "Move!" he commanded. Centurion snorted and bent his head to drink.

Theo suddenly became aware of amused looks as the soldiers forded the river on either side of him. He dropped Centurion's reins and waded to shore.

"Stay here with the stubborn beast, then, and catch up to me when he chooses." He gathered up the reins of their ponies and stormed off down the path.

He had expected that they would make camp after crossing the river, but the signal came back to forge on.

"We must conserve our supplies," the count told him. "All the ports from here on are in Fatimid hands and we can expect no further reprovisioning. Bohemond is anxious to press on with as little delay as possible."

Emma and Centurion did not rejoin him until evening.

"He refused to move until the entire army finished crossing," Emma said, with a rueful shake of her head. "But he is much refreshed now."

They drew near to Beirut. Theo marveled at the lavish city, and the luxuriousness of the gardens and orchards surrounding it. Instead of rocky shoreline, he saw vast beaches of sand. Truly, Beirut seemed like a paradise, set on the shores of the gleaming sea. The citizens of the city, at first fearful, began tentatively to come out of their houses as the army passed. Bearing gifts of fruit and all kinds of food, they pressed the offerings onto the crusaders.

"We are guaranteed safe passage through the city if we do no harm to the fruit trees, crops or vines," Godfrey told them. The order was passed down through the ranks. The troops obeyed, and the passage became a kind of celebration. The townsfolk came out laughing, carrying armfuls and baskets of food; the crusaders accepted it all with delight.

The next town on the coast was Sidon. Here, the

garrison made a sortie against the crusaders. The army repulsed it easily and, in retaliation, the troops were let loose to plunder and ravage the gardens of the suburbs. Then they moved quickly on to Tyre.

"We will rest here," Bohemond finally decreed. So they made camp outside the high walls of the city.

Theo could see soldiers from the town's garrison spying on them from behind the safety of the walls, but none came out.

† † †

If Beirut had seemed a paradise, Tyre was even more beautiful. Emma tethered Centurion in the shade of a wide-branching tree where the breeze from the sea could help cool him. Although it was still only May, the weather was already hot. Theo was entranced by the sandstone houses of the city that glistened pink and amber in the sun. The town was set comfortably among fields and groves, with the sea on one side and thickly wooded mountains rising on the other, some still snow-capped. Rivers of blossoms from countless orchards cascaded down through the valley that cleft the hills above them.

"I must go exploring," Emma declared the morning after they had made camp. "Will you go with me?"

"Exploring," Theo questioned. "Where?"

"Up there." She pointed to the trees rising up the hillside above them.

"But the camp—the beasts—we cannot leave them unattended for so long."

"I know a boy who will watch them for us and make certain Centurion stays in the shade and has plenty of water. He's the son of a friend of mine."

"You seem to have made a lot of strange friends," Theo answered. "Is this the friend who taught you how to use the bow and arrow?"

Emma flushed. "Yes," she said. "He is one of the archers. You do not know him."

"Does this friend know you are not really mute? That you are not a boy?"

"He does not."

"How did you manage that?"

Emma shrugged. "I managed." She would say no more.

Theo looked up at the cool darkness of the woods, the inviting flash of small streams among the fruit blossoms. He gave up the questioning. It did not matter. "Get your boy, then, and we'll go," he said. "It's a good idea."

They made their way out of the camp, Emma following behind Theo with her hood pulled low over her face as if she were a dutiful groom attending to his master. As they reached the outskirts, they were hailed by a shout. Theo looked back to see Amalric coming after them.

"Where are you going?" he called.

"Exploring. Up in the hills," Emma answered. "Will you come with us?"

Amalric hesitated. He looked at Theo.

Theo grinned. "I echo my groom's invitation," he said.

Amalric shrugged, and made up his mind. "All right," he said, "I'll come." He fell into step beside Theo. Emma followed.

They climbed toward the wood through fields bright with purple asters, sweet-smelling clover, daisies and scarlet-petaled anemones. In the distance, they could hear bleating and the occasional tinny ring of goat bells. Past orchards heavy with the scent of oranges and lemons, past silver-leaved olive trees, higher and higher they clambered. The air was cooler here, crisp and clean.

Once out of sight of the camp, Emma could control her eagerness no longer and raced to lead the way. She climbed at such a pace that Theo and Amalric, although they would never admit it, began to find it hard to catch their breath. Finally, she stopped at the mouth of what seemed to be a small cave. She dropped down to sit on a rocky outcropping, and faced back the way they had come.

"Look!" she exclaimed.

Theo and Amalric threw themselves on the ground at her feet, and looked where she was pointing. Below them, behind its walls, the city of Tyre lay spread out to their view. Gray marble streets, as ancient as history, dissected it neatly and formally. Flat-topped houses, minarets, domes slumbered among the fronds of palm trees as if stunned by the heat of the sun that beat down upon them. At the shoreline, rows of pure white columns, their original purpose lost in the memory of time, stretched from the city out into the sea itself. From here, they could see, through the crystal-clear turquoise water, more columns broken and scattered in the sand on the bottom, as if cast there by a giant hand. Fishing boats sailed over and among them. In the eastern part of the city was a ruin piled high with Roman bricks; in the west, strange to their eyes, a vast circular amphitheater, ringed with rows of seats.

"I've heard tales of those places," Theo said. "In olden times, the Romans forced Christians to fight within them—with each other, with other men and with fearsome beasts."

A stream cascaded in a foam of white off the edge of a cliff far above them. Too far away for them to hear, the water fell into a silver ribbon that wound its way past them and on into the valley below.

They sat for a long while in companionable silence. Amalric, ever restless, busied his hands with the making of a wreath out of the meadow flowers around him.

When Theo finally turned to look back at Emma, he saw that the stones she sat on were part of a terrace built by human hands. The cave behind her was flanked with more stones. From where he sat, he could see markings on them. He got to his feet and walked over to examine them more closely.

"What is it?" Emma asked. "What have you found?"

"These marks," Theo answered, "they look like writing, but of a sort I have never seen before."

Emma was on her feet in an instant to join him. "They are on either side of the cave," she said, tracing them with her fingertips. "I wonder if there are more inside?" She made as if to go in.

"Wait," Amalric called. He leaped to his feet as well and caught up to her, the wreath in his hand. He lifted it up and placed it upon her head. "A crown, my lady."

Emma smiled. She had thrown her hood back. Her hair had grown out somewhat, and the flowers glowed crimson against the black curls that framed her face.

"I thank you, my lord," she answered, dropping him a curtsy.

He responded with a deep bow of his own and an answering smile.

"At your service, madam."

Emma turned back to the cave with a flourish worthy of a queen, and walked into it.

"Take care—" Theo began, but his words were drowned out by a cry.

"Oh, Theo!"

He ran in, then skidded to a halt. The sun struck the far wall, lighting up a throne carved into the rock. Two monstrous beasts, heavily maned and baring their teeth, flanked either side of it. Their long, tufted tails curled around them to meet at the base.

"This must be a temple," Emma cried. "An ancient, pagan temple!" Queenly dignity forgotten, she ran across to the throne, pulled herself up and sat on it, one hand on each of the beasts' heads. She lifted her flower-crowned head high. A shaft of sunlight limned her with brightness.

"Emma!" Theo was appalled. Heathen though the temple was, Emma's brazenness seemed like sacrilege.

"A goddess. A goddess summoning her slaves to do her bidding."

Amalric's voice came mocking from the opening of the grotto.

Seventeen

At that moment, the sun dimmed, and the cave was plunged into gloom. "I like this not at all," Theo said. He made the sign of the cross. "Let us get out of here."

Emma laughed. "For shame, a Christian knight afraid of the old gods."

"I am not afraid," Theo said. "But this place has an evil feel to it. We should get back into the clean air."

When they emerged, they found that dark clouds were fast covering the sun. The rumble of thunder rolled out. In the distance, lightning flashed; they watched it strike first one hilltop, then another. The sudden change from the bright, sunlit day was so dramatic that they stood watching the approaching storm as if mesmerized.

"We are going to be drenched," Theo said finally, wrenching his gaze away from the spectacle. "We must hurry."

They started down, but the rain caught them on the outskirts of the camp. Emma led the way, laughing and excited by the storm. The sudden onslaught of the downpour only seemed to exhilarate her all the more. Her crown of flowers shredded; wet petals glued themselves to her forehead. Her cheeks were flushed, her eyes bright. She had flung back her cloak and her tunic clung wetly to her body.

At that moment, Guy emerged from the trees. He stopped when he saw them, eyes fixed, wide with astonishment, on Emma.

Emma grabbed the folds of her cloak and wrapped them around her. Her hands searched desperately for the hood to cover her face, but it was too late.

Guy recovered his voice. He began to laugh.

"So this is your groom! And I suspected it not when I saved her life. Baldwin's wench! Truly, Theo, I would not have thought you capable of such a trick."

"You don't understand—" Theo began.

"Oh, but of course I do. I only wonder that you allowed such a delightful toy to play at war. You might well have lost her."

"She is not—"

Guy interrupted Theo. "What an interesting situation," he said. "I wonder what I should do with it."

Before Theo could answer, he turned and left. His laughter rang out behind him, loud and scornful.

† † †

Theo lay sleepless in his tent that night. He had heard rumors that Baldwin, who had established his own little kingdom in Edessa, was thinking of riding down to rejoin the crusade, now that the army was so close to Jerusalem. If he did, and Guy spoke out—and why would he not?—Baldwin was certain to demand Emma's return. What would they do? Theo was certain of one thing only: he would not let Baldwin get his hands on Emma again. But how could Theo oppose him? His own foster father would be shocked at what he had done. The count would be certain to side with Baldwin.

Theo tossed restlessly on his pallet, turning the questions over and over in his mind. He had barely dozed off into a fitful sleep when a sudden, muffled cry awoke him. He leaped up and dashed outside. The cry had come from Emma's tent. As he ran toward it, he saw the small shelter wobble. The sides seemed to bulge for a moment, and then a figure scrambled out through the opening, on his hands and knees. Guy was backing out as quickly as he could, followed by Emma, who was wielding a stick of firewood and beating him on the head and shoulders. She was swearing in almost every dialect to be heard in the camp.

Theo began to go to her aid, then stopped. His help wasn't needed. Guy managed to get to his feet, and for a moment it seemed as if he would attack Emma, but she stood her ground, brandishing her weapon.

Theo could hold back no longer. This time, it was he who laughed.

Guy whipped around.

"I think you will keep our secret now," Theo chortled, "or the entire camp will be delighted to hear the story of how a maid beat you off with a stick of firewood. It would cause many an hour of merriment, I vow."

"You!" Guy's eyes darkened. "You have made one mistake too many, my friend."

Theo sobered immediately. His hand went to the dagger at his belt.

"Take care that *you* do not make a mistake," he said, his voice suddenly ice-cold. Emma stared at him in surprise. "The maid is under my care. When the crusade is over, we are to be wed. You will not harm her in any way."

"I do not take orders from you," Guy spat. He whipped out his dagger and lunged toward Theo.

Not quickly enough. Theo met the other knight's charge with a slashing blow that slit open the sleeve of Guy's tunic and drew blood. Guy's dagger dropped to the ground. Theo placed a foot on it and faced him.

"One word from you about her true identity, and I will inform Duke Godfrey of your assault upon her. The duke punishes most harshly those who commit the crime of rape, as you know. Punishment and ridicule will be your reward if you do not keep quiet about this. Not only will the story be told of how you could not master a mere maid, but I will be glad to inform anyone who asks how you came by that wound on your arm." Theo bent to retrieve Guy's dagger. He tossed it carelessly from one hand to the other. "And I will take delight in showing them your dagger as proof."

Guy faced Theo, his face contorted with rage, his fists clenched as if he would attack Theo barehanded. Then he spat again.

"You will pay for this!" Guy whirled around and strode off.

"We are to wed?" The words were spoken in a light, mocking tone, but Emma's voice shook slightly. "May I ask when you intended to inform me of this decision?"

Theo looked at her across the campfire, at a loss now for words. "I did not know myself," he brought out, finally. "It seems my tongue has spoken of its own accord and told what my heart is feeling."

"You would marry me?"

"I would." And then he knew, suddenly and completely, that marrying Emma was all he wanted in the world. He was at her side in two quick steps. "When you were wounded . . . When I thought you might

217

die . . . I truly did not know how I could go on living without you. Will you—when the crusade is done—will you wed me?"

He reached out, almost fearfully, and took her face between his hands. He rubbed gently at a smudge of dirt on her cheek. One strand of hair curled down over her eyes, and he brushed it back. She looked up at him, then dropped her head to his chest. He encircled her with his arms and drew her close. Her body relaxed into his embrace. For a moment, he could feel the soft warmth of her, and then she stiffened. She raised her eyes to his once more.

"Ask me again, Theo," she whispered. "When all this is over . . . if it is ever over . . . if we two are still alive . . . ask me again, then." She reached up to touch his cheek, then slipped back into her tent and pulled the door flap closed behind her.

Theo built the fire up. He sat beside it until the first pale streaks of dawn began to lighten the sky.

☦   ☦   ☦

After that, Theo insisted that Emma set her tent up at night immediately beside his. He would have had her move her pallet right into his tent, but she refused. During the day, he kept close by her as much as possible. He could not forget the look in Guy's eyes. The man was poisoned with hate; Theo knew he would take his revenge somehow.

They left Tyre and marched on down the coast to Acre. There, the governor pressed more gifts of fruits and food upon them, ensuring the safety of the fertile farms in his territory. They proceeded to Haifa and on, under the shadow of Mount Carmel, until they finally reached southern Caesarea.

"We are to stay here for four days in order to celebrate Whitsun properly," he told Emma, as he returned to camp after breaking his fast with the count. There had been a shyness between them since Guy's attack, but neither of them had been able to speak of it. Nor did they speak of Theo's declaration. Jerusalem was only a week's travel away. The final battle loomed. Time enough, then, to think of themselves.

At the end of the celebration, they set out again, inland this time, following an old road that led away from the coast and wound upwards into the Judean hills. As they traveled, it grew even hotter. The sun blazed down upon them out of cloudless skies. The land was changing; there were fewer and fewer trees to provide shade. Emma trailed behind Theo, both walking to save their horses' strength. The Turkish ponies managed well enough, but Centurion was in trouble.

"Theo," Emma called, low, so that no one else should hear. It was noon of the second day after they had begun the climb inland.

Theo turned to her, wiping sweat out of his eyes. His tunic stuck to his back, and small flying insects tormented him.

"It is Centurion. He can go no farther. We must rest."

"Ramleh is close before us," Theo called back. "We can rest there. There will be shade and water for him."

"I know not whether he will make it," Emma answered. There was a note of desperation in her voice.

Theo stopped and came back to look more closely at the huge warhorse. He pulled their ponies and pack animals to one side to let those behind pass them by. Centurion took two more steps, as if unaware that his masters had halted. His eyes were glazed and unseeing. His breathing came in ragged, sucking gasps. Emma tugged gently on his halter to stop him. He came to a halt and stood, his immense body swaying slightly, head hanging down. Sweat foamed on his neck and withers and ran in streams to drip off his belly onto the ground. Flies clustered around his eyes, but he seemed oblivious to them. As they watched, he gave a convulsive shudder. Emma reached for a skin of water and held it out to him. He ignored it. She brushed the flies away.

"We cannot go on, Theo. He is going to die if he does not rest. This heat is too much for him."

Theo did not answer. Of the huge warhorses that had left the Ardennes, Centurion was the last one left. The others had succumbed to the rigors of the journey long ago, or had been left in the towns they had passed through when the horses had become too exhausted to go farther. Theo had clung to the possibility that Centurion's enormous strength and force of will would carry him through. Now, it seemed, he had reached the end.

"We will rest awhile," Theo said.

No matter how much she coaxed, however, Emma could not get Centurion to drink. He had stopped eating days ago. She picked up a coarse piece of sacking and began to rub him down. She scratched his belly thoroughly with a brush made of twigs. He shivered from time to time, but otherwise seemed insensible to her ministrations. His breathing became even more labored. Finally, Emma stopped and just leaned her head lightly against his neck. With one hand, she caressed the woolly gray hair of his mane; with the other, she rubbed his forehead on the spot where she knew he liked it best.

Theo watched. He rebuked her not for spoiling the horse, nor for treating him in an undignified manner.

Suddenly, Centurion tossed his head, knocking Emma aside. For one moment, his eyes cleared and he looked full at her, and then they dulled. One last convulsive shudder shook the massive frame and, with a ground-jarring thud, he fell. His breathing stopped.

Emma threw herself upon him. Tears streamed down her face, mingling with sweat and dirt. Theo knelt beside her. He would have put an arm around her, to comfort her, but the steady stream of curious crusaders and pilgrims passing by precluded any show of tenderness toward one who was supposed to be his groom. He laid a hand on the warhorse's head.

"So, after all, you will not be there to carry me into Jerusalem," he said. His voice broke. "I shall miss you, my old friend."

† † †

They left Centurion by the roadside. There was nothing else they could do. The birds of prey began to circle high above almost before they had traveled out of sight.

It was night before Theo and Emma reached the town of Ramleh. There they found the crusaders already comfortably installed. The inhabitants had fled the town in terror at the news of their coming, but only after destroying the great Church of St. George that had stood in the ruined village of Lydda on Ramleh's outskirts.

They rested there for three days, the crusaders exulted by the taking of a Muslim town in the heart of the Holy Land. Only Theo and Emma took no part in the celebrations. The death of Centurion was too much with them. On the fourth day, the army resumed its march on Jerusalem.

The crusaders traveled all day and on through the night. The wooded hillside gradually gave way to stony, red-earthed slopes, shaded only by stunted trees and bushes. The alien nature of this new land began to exert a strange kind of hold on the crusaders.

"It is so barren," Emma whispered. "It chills my soul."

There was an eclipse of the moon that night. While the crusaders marched, they watched in awe as the moon dwindled to a crescent, and then was blacked out completely.

"It is an omen," the priests told them as they halted briefly for mass the next morning. "It portends the eclipse of the Crescent of Islam itself."

But their words brought no reassurance to the crusaders. They pressed on in an ever-increasing silence.

Theo turned once to look back at the procession. How few we are compared to the vast army that set out from Constantinople, he thought. Hardly more than a thousand knights were left, and fewer than half the foot soldiers remained. How many pilgrims had died, Theo could only guess. Certainly, there were not nearly as many straggling in at night as there had been. It was a sad and dispirited army that trailed behind him now—a ghost of the glorious crusade that had set out so triumphantly to do God's will almost three long years ago.

Before noon on the seventh day of June, the vanguard of the army—Theo, Emma and Amalric included—reached the summit of the road at the mosque of the prophet Samuel, on the hilltop that the pilgrims called Montjoie, the Hill of Joy.

There, before them, stood Jerusalem. Theo dropped to his knees. All around him, nobles and soldiers alike were doing the same.

Jerusalem! God's own city. At last!

MEDITERRANEAN SEA

Jerusalem

EGYPT

Eighteen

Theo sat beside his campfire, staring at the city. God's own city—but it was also one of the greatest fortresses in the world, secure behind its formidable walls and towers. The crusaders had been deployed and were ready to begin the siege. Godfrey's troops had been assigned the northwest side of the city as far down as the Jaffa Gate. Beside the gate, directly in front of Theo, was the citadel, the Tower of David. Its bulk loomed against the dying light of the day. Cicadas shrilled in the scraggly cypress

224

trees behind him. Small, swift birds darted in the twilight. Smells of cooking wafted out to the crusaders' camp from the other side of the walls, amid the sounds of a city settling itself for the night. Calls, cries, the wail of thin, strange-sounding music. Firelight flickered through the slit-holes of the citadel and the other towers, where Theo knew the Egyptian Fatimid soldiers stood guard—staring at the crusaders, even as the crusaders stared at them.

"The governor is Iftikhar ad-Dawla," Godfrey told his troops. "An experienced and well-seasoned soldier. He has had ample warning of our coming and has used the time to strengthen his walls. He has driven all the flocks and herds into the city, and the city is well supplied with cisterns for water. He is prepared for a long siege."

Theo had wondered at the absence of animals and herders in the hills as they had approached. The duke's words explained it.

The next morning, he was worried to find Emma gone from the campsite when he stumbled out of his tent. He became uneasy now whenever she was out of his sight. The sun was just beginning to send streaks of color through the sky, and a mist lay heavy in the valleys around them.

"Please God she doesn't get into any more trouble," he muttered, as he gathered sticks and twigs for a fire. Very little on this bare hillside could be used for fuel. That is going to be a problem very soon, Theo thought. He rationed out oats for the horses, but there was no water. Another problem. Perhaps that was where Emma was—fetching water from the nearest well.

The sun rose. A pitiless, blazing orb, it burned off the mists below and drained the blue out of the sky above with the intensity of its heat. Theo moved the horses into what little shade the sparse trees provided, but they stamped their feet restlessly and tossed their heads back and forth. They ate only half the food Theo had given them, even though he had skimped on their usual portion. It was obvious they were thirsty. Where was Emma?

He had almost decided to go and look for her when she reappeared. She staggered under the weight of two buckets of water, one dangling on either end of a stick she had slung across her shoulders. Her face was bright red under her hood and running with sweat. Theo hastened to take the buckets from her.

"Iftikhar . . . He has poisoned or filled in all the wells outside the walls," she panted. "The dog! Mind you, I would have done so myself if I'd been in his position, but it's annoying just the same." She dropped to the ground beside the tiny fire. "There is only one good well left and it's away around by the south wall. I managed to fill our buckets, but the soldiers on the walls jeered at me the whole time I was doing it. Could just as well have been arrows rather than words, though, so I think myself rather fortunate."

"Our only source of water is within bow range of the walls?" Theo asked incredulously.

"I'm afraid so," Emma answered.

"We will have to find a river . . . a stream . . ." Theo looked around him. The few trees that grew on these stony hills did not provide nearly enough shade. Even this early in the morning, the heat was intense. A breeze had sprung up, but it gave no relief. If possible, it was hotter than the still air, and only made their discomfort worse.

"We will not be able to hold out here for long," Theo said. "This siege must be short. We must take Jerusalem quickly, or we will die."

† † †

Godfrey planned an attack the next week. As usual, Theo fought side by side with Amalric. Together, as the mangonels and catapults bombarded the walls with boulders and stones, they swarmed up the ladders behind the duke and Count Garnier. They charged the soldiers at the top, overrunning them with the ferocity and desperation of their attack. For a time, Theo thought they might have a chance of success. Then he heard Godfrey call for a retreat.

Back down the ladders they scrambled, in a frenzy of panic and humiliation. The Egyptian soldiers poured liquid fire down upon them as they fled. Theo had heard of Greek fire, as it was called, but had never seen it and had not really believed in it. But as the rivers of oily flame cascaded down onto the soldiers still on the ladders, the screams of the burned men proved its existence only too well.

"We had too few ladders and too few engines of war. Too few of our men were able to storm the walls," Godfrey told them at their council that night. "If we are to take Jerusalem, we must wage an all-out attack. We need more siege machines, more mangonels, battering rams and ladders, many, many more. We must attack from as many positions as possible. All of us—all at once!"

There was a general murmur of agreement, then one dissenting voice.

"Where are we to get the wood to build these machines, my lord? There is barely enough here to feed our fires. And what of the nails and bolts for fitting them together?"

"There are forests around Samaria. Tancred, you and Robert of Flanders, take your men and cut down trees. Take the camels—they are by far the best beasts of burden in this heat and need next to no water. As for the rest of us—we will pray that supplies come from the coast. In the meantime, we build. All of us."

Theo and Amalric worked with the rest. Emma did her share as well. Princes worked side by side with pilgrims. Women and children worked from sun-up to nightfall. Tancred and Robert came back laden with rough-hewn logs and planks. Theo helped to tear wagons apart for the nails and bolts, and then the army burned the wagons for fuel. The lack of water was deadly, however. Pack animals and herds they had captured along the way began to die of thirst in large numbers.

"At least they provide food," Amalric remarked cynically.

Godfrey sent out detachments from the camp every day to find streams and wells. They were guided by native Christians who had been turned out of the city and had joined the crusaders. Some even went as far as the Jordan River to find water. The well Emma had found the first day—the Pool of Siloam, the Jerusalem Christians called it—was deep and brimming with cool, clear water, but the sentries on the walls had left off taunting and had settled down to killing all who came near it.

The hot breeze Theo had felt the first day outside the walls of Jerusalem became a steady wind. Dry and burning, it laid a fine film of sand and dust on everything and everyone in the camp. It never ceased, and it drove men and women crazy.

"Many of the crusaders are undergoing baptism in the river Jordan, gathering palm branches from the riverbank and deserting," Theo told Emma.

"I know," she answered. "This is not what they expected. They feel we will never conquer Jerusalem." She looked at the walls towering above them. "They think we will die here."

They might be right, Theo thought, and thrust the unbidden idea out of his mind immediately.

A few days later, Amalric barged into their camp with news.

"Six Christian ships have put into Jaffa. Their scouts arrived at the camp last night. They have supplies! Food, ropes, nails, bolts—everything we need!"

"Now, we can really build," Godfrey announced at their evening conference. "And as well as everything else, I will build a siege castle, as high as the walls themselves. Higher! A tower set on wheels that we can roll right up to the walls. Then we can attack from within the tower without the need of ladders. We'll fit it out with catapults as well." He strode back and forth, his tall figure seeming to fill the tent.

"We can fight with fire, too," he added. His eyes blazed and he flung his long, fair hair back with an impatient toss of his head. "I have Christians here who escaped the city and have brought the secret of the Greek fire with them. We can hurl it down upon the Egyptians from the tower and the mangonels can send it flying over the walls." He turned to Gaston of Béarn. "Build the castle well out of sight of the fort. It will be a surprise to the garrison, and not a very welcome one, I warrant." He laughed, a sound that had not been heard in his tent for many months. His eagerness and enthusiasm were infectious. Amalric thumped Theo on the back with such gleeful force as they left the meeting that it knocked the breath out of him.

But the work went slowly, and they suffered terribly from the heat. In spite of their leaders' assurances, more and more people deserted every day. Then Theo heard news that a great army had set out from Egypt to relieve Jerusalem.

"The mood in the camp is desperate," he told Emma. "The priest, Peter Desiderius, says we must do something. He is calling for three holy days of fasting. He says Bishop Adhemar himself appeared to him, and told him we must hold a fast and then walk barefoot around Jerusalem. Only then will we be able to gather our forces and attack."

"Once again, when we are starving, they call for a fast," Emma muttered. "These priests do have a sense of humor."

† † †

They fasted for three days, but did not cease to work. On the Friday of that week, the procession formed. Theo and Amalric lined themselves up with their lords behind the bishops and the priests, who carried the crosses and holy relics they had brought all this way with them. The foot soldiers and pilgrims followed; Emma, in her groom's garb, chose to walk with them.

Theo was lightheaded from the heat and the lack of food. He was barely aware of the soldiers and townsfolk who gathered on the walls to mock them. He kept his eyes on the ground, concentrating only on putting one foot ahead of the other. He tried to follow the prayers of the priests, but a buzzing in his head drowned out their chanting. They circled the city, then climbed the Mount of Olives. There, the priests began to preach.

"We are here!" Arnulf of Rhohes proclaimed. "We are outside the walls of Jerusalem itself!" He was widely acknowledged to be the finest preacher in the army, and a silence fell on the vast crowd as they listened intently to him. "We have followed God's will and done His bidding, and now we are at the gates of the holiest of His cities. Will you not rejoice? Will you not look within your hearts and find the strength for one last battle? One last battle, and then our glorious crusade will be ended. God's will *will* have been done!"

As the priest spoke, Theo saw heads around him begin to lift. The dullness began to clear from people's eyes.

Peter the Hermit rose next. Forgotten by all was his inglorious defeat at Civetot, his attempt to desert the crusade at Antioch. As he preached, his eyes blazed with their old intensity. His voice rolled over the hilltop. After so many months, he spoke most of the dialects heard around the camp—translators were quick to interpret his words into the others. The people began to murmur, and then to shout. They raised their fists to the sky and shook them at the very walls of Jerusalem itself.

"We *will* conquer. God wills it! God wills it!"

The old battle cry of the crusade rang out, and echoed back and back again from the surrounding hills.

Theo found himself shouting with the rest. Gone was the lightheadedness, gone the weakness. The clamor of the multitude surrounded him and filled him with strength.

"God wills it!" he cried. "God wills it!"

† † †

During the next two days, Theo and the crusaders returned to their work with renewed fervor. Even the oldest of men and women did their part, sewing ox-hide and camel-hide onto the exposed woodwork on the siege machines to protect it from the Greek fire.

"Raymond of Toulouse is building a second siege castle," the count announced. "It is also being built out of sight of the city walls. We will have some surprises for our enemy, never fear."

By the second week in July, the siege castles were ready.

"Now," Godfrey commanded. "Let us wheel them out of hiding!"

Theo and Amalric pulled on their castle, shoulder to shoulder with the count and Godfrey himself, along with dozens of their men. It was an enormous tower. At first, the wheels refused to turn. The struggle to get the castle into motion seemed impossible. Theo felt the veins in his forehead swell with the effort. Beside him, Amalric swore as his foot slipped and he almost fell. Then, slowly, cumbersomely, the tower began to move, up the hillside, and down the slight decline on the other side. Then up to face the northern wall, where startled faces were beginning to show themselves over the tops of the battlements. To the south, Theo knew that Raymond and his men were setting his castle into position. A third, smaller one would be set against the northwest corner.

Theo wiped the sweat from his eyes. He straightened. The battle for Jerusalem was about to begin.

MEDITERRANEAN SEA

Jerusalem

EGYPT

Nineteen

Their first task was to fill in the ditch that prevented the siege castles from being placed right up against the city walls, but the work was dangerous. As soon as the Egyptians saw the castles approaching, they began to bombard them. Theo worked side by side with Amalric and Emma. It seemed to him that everyone in the crusade had turned out to help, in spite of the deadly rain of stones and liquid fire. The sun burned down upon them out of a cloudless sky.

Theo stopped briefly to rest around midday. He looked up and was amazed to see the heat-shimmering air alive with color. He passed a hand over his eyes, certain his brain was crazed by the sun, and then realized he was surrounded by brilliant, multi-hued butterflies. He reached out to touch Emma's arm.

"Look," he croaked. His throat was parched and dry, his head pounding with pain. The butterflies darted and swooped in a sun-mad, dizzy-making dance all their own.

Emma straightened up and leaned on her shovel. A butterfly alighted on the handle. She stared at it, dazed, as if unable to make sense of it. Then she raised her eyes. For several long minutes the butterflies danced; then, obeying some mysterious signal obvious only to them, all flew off. A boulder crashed to the ground beside Theo and Emma. They flinched, ducked, and began to dig again.

On the morning of the next day, they pulled Godfrey's tower over the filled-in ditch. Theo had time only to grasp Emma's hand for a brief second.

"Stay safe, Theo," she whispered, and then she and the other pilgrims ran back out of range of the missiles being hurled from atop the walls.

Theo saw Godfrey himself, oblivious to the lethal hail all around him, standing tall and proud on the top story as they pushed the castle the last few meters. Immediately, crusader soldiers began to bombard the wall with boulders and clay pots filled with Greek fire.

The assault was returned in full force by the Fatimid soldiers manning the walls. As soon as the castle touched, a swarm of engineers set about making a bridge between it and the top of the wall, while a steady stream of arrows from Godfrey's archers held off the Egyptians.

While the bridge was being finished, Theo waited with Amalric and the other knights in the enclosed bottom half of the tower. The press of men in the gloom was great; the smell of sweat and fear almost overpowering. They could not see what was happening outside, but all around them the battle raged. The tower shook with the shock of the catapults every time they fired on the top stage. It shuddered every time it took a hit from the opposing army. The smell of burning hide began to seep into where the knights waited. Several men cried out; panic was not far away. Theo felt Amalric's shoulder press against his own and he took comfort from it. Both were wearing their mail-ringed leather armor, necessary for the fighting to come, but its heaviness added to the heat and discomfort. The waiting was almost unbearable. Theo felt stomach-churning, almost overwhelming fear. Far better was the crashing, chaotic charge on horseback, with trumpets blaring and war-cries echoing all around. In battle, there was no time to think—no time to imagine your own death waiting for you.

A roar from above was followed by a sudden wave of movement. Theo found himself scrambling for the ladder that led to the upper story. Men behind him shouted and pushed forward. When he reached the upper level, sunlight blinded him for a moment. Then he saw Godfrey standing on the wall on the other side of the bridge, waving them on. He pulled his sword from its scabbard and raced across.

"The gate, Theo!" Count Garnier was at his side. "We must open the gate for the rest of the army!"

Theo followed him, bounding down steps carved into the stone wall. At the bottom, the gate stood, barred and bolted. The Fatimid guards drew their swords. Theo charged the nearest one and their weapons crossed with a jarring clang. His opponent drew back and struck again, but his sword glanced off Theo's shield. At the same moment, Theo struck at the man's unguarded side and felt his sword sink deep. He pulled back and the man fell off it. A froth of blood spewed from his mouth and he lay still at Theo's feet. Theo whirled to face the others, but they lay sprawled around him in slowly widening pools of blood. The count and two of his men were already tugging at the heavy crossbar that sealed the gate. Theo leaped over the body of the soldier he had slain and raced to help. They slid the crossbar free, but before they could open the gate, it was pushed wide by the press of people on the other side. Theo jumped aside to avoid the foot soldiers, who were the first to burst through, and then, to his amazement, he saw a horde of pilgrims—men, women, even children—

come rushing through after them. Armed with cudgels, sticks and shovels, they poured through, screaming hate and defiance, maddened beyond belief after weeks of starvation and heat, years of pain and sacrifice. The defenders of the city fell back before them.

All of a sudden, Amalric was at his side again.

"Theo!" he shouted, and pointed.

Theo looked. A group of Egyptian soldiers was running for a mosque.

"After them!" Amalric cried, and set off in pursuit.

They caught up with them at the mosque door. Theo saw the gleam of a scimitar flash down toward him. He parried, but the scimitar faltered and the soldier screamed as Amalric's sword struck first.

This battle was short. A crowd of crusaders rushed to join them; the Muslims were soon slain. For a moment, there was chaos as pilgrims poured in as well, wielding their makeshift weapons. Then another band of Fatimid defenders was sighted.

"Kill them!" a voice screamed, and the crowd swarmed in their direction.

Suddenly, Theo heard a cry from behind him.

"Theo!"

He felt a searing pain streak down his back. He whirled around. Guy stood there, sword raised, dripping blood, poised to strike again. Theo raised his own sword to defend himself, but Guy's eyes were wide with shock. His arm fell, and the sword dropped from his hand. He stared at Theo a second longer with a puzzled, uncomprehending look, then slowly toppled forward. A dagger was embedded in his back.

Only then did Theo see Emma. Her eyes were fixed on the dying man. She looked up to meet Theo's stare. Her hands were at her sides, held out in an oddly imploring gesture.

"He was going to kill you," she whispered. "I had to kill him first."

Then the world turned black, and Theo fell across Guy's body.

✝   ✝   ✝

He regained consciousness slowly. First, he became aware that he was lying on cold stone, on his stomach. His back was afire with pain. It was dark, but he seemed to be in a protected place. There were walls all around him. From somewhere outside, he could hear noises. Screams. He turned his head. Now he could see a rectangle that must be a window, lit by flames from without. More screams. As he came back to full consciousness, they became louder. A figure moved past the rectangle of light. Theo tensed and tried to sit up. Pain roared through his body and he whirlpooled back down into dizziness.

"Theo? Are you awake? Oh, thanks be to God. I thought you were dying." It was Emma's voice, but thin, on the verge of hysteria.

He fought to speak. "What's happening? How goes the battle?"

"The battle is over."

"But those screams . . ."

"They are people—people being murdered. Oh, Theo, it is like a vision of hell itself out there! I dragged you here, and then I tried to go and find help for you, but the crusaders . . ." She dropped to her knees on the stone beside him. In the flickering light, he saw her bury her face in her hands. "They have gone mad, Theo. All of them. They are killing everyone they can catch. Men, women . . . I saw a knight strike down a child, Theo! A child!" Her voice broke. Sobs racked her body.

Theo clenched his teeth and rolled onto his side. He reached out and managed to touch her.

"Lie beside me, Emma."

She burrowed into him; he wrapped his arms around her.

He held her all through the rest of that terrible night. Emma could not stop shaking. She shuddered with every scream from the street outside.

By the time the dawn sent tentative fingers of light through the window, the screams had stopped and Emma finally lay quiet in Theo's arms. He thought she slept and dared not move in case he wakened her, but his back was torturing him. Then Emma spoke.

"I must go and find help for you, Theo."

"You cannot go out there alone."

Emma sat up. In the early morning dimness, he could see only the dead-white oval of her face. Theo sat, too, but could not suppress a moan of pain.

"It is quiet. It is all over. I will be safe."

Before Theo could make a move to stop her, she had risen to her feet and disappeared. He made a futile attempt to get up and follow her, then sank back into unconsciousness.

He woke again to the sound of two voices: Emma's and another's. The alcove where he lay was light now; he recognized the man who followed her in as one of the crusaders' healers, a man well known for his skill and compassion. He carried bandages and a skin of water. With Emma's help, he cleansed and bound Theo's wound. By the time he had finished and left to tend to the many others who awaited him, Theo's head had cleared and he felt steadier. He sat up. Emma was standing by the window, staring out.

"They killed them all." Her voice was so low at first he thought he had misunderstood her.

"All?"

"All," Emma repeated. "All afternoon, all through the night, they killed. They spared no one. A band of Muslims took shelter in one of the mosques after surrendering to Tancred. His banner flew above them, to protect them, but our glorious crusaders broke in and slew every one of them."

Theo started to say something. She silenced him with an abrupt motion.

"The Jews, Theo. All the Jews in the city fled to their synagogue. The crusaders set it on fire and burned everyone within. There is not a Muslim or Jewish man, woman or child left alive. The streets are piled with their bodies." Her voice was toneless with the horror of what she had seen and what she had heard. "The victory is complete, Theo. Jerusalem is once again a Christian city. They will say mass this morning in this very church."

Theo struggled to his feet. Ignoring the pain that shot down into his legs and threatened to collapse them beneath him, he walked over to Emma and stood beside her. She turned to him. Her eyes were dark. Dead.

"What have we done, Theo?" she whispered. "What have we done?"

† † †

Theo and Emma attended the mass. The nave of the church was filled to capacity. Some of the nobles and the leaders had managed to find time to cleanse themselves of the blood of battle, and were dressed with as much pomp and finery as they could assemble, but most were still as blood-stained and filthy as Theo and Emma. Emma had protested at Theo's going, fearing he was too weak, but he had insisted. The walk from the alcove to the nave where the service took place was only a short one, but he was sweating and weak by the time they arrived. They found a stone for him to sit on at the back of the church.

Duke Godfrey sat at the right hand of the priest, Peter Desiderius. Count Garnier stood behind him. The count caught sight of Theo and his face lightened with relief.

"God's will has been done. We gather here victorious in His sight." The priest's words rolled out around the gathering. There was no wild exultation, however, only a heavy silence. The heads of all in the congregation bowed as the priest blessed them. From outside, the sound of the streets being cleared filtered into the silent assembly. Huge pyres of bodies were being piled up in every vacant lot and set on fire. An oath rang out, shocking the silence with its vulgarity. Theo moved slightly, then flinched. His back felt as if it were being torn apart. The wound inflicted by Guy's sword was superficial and would heal well, the healer had said. But inside Theo, as the smell of the burning bodies seeped into the church, a far deeper wound festered.

† † †

Theo sat in the garden of a small house on the outskirts of Jerusalem. It was a house he had purchased from a Christian of the city who had wanted to journey to Antioch. He knew very well that Emma would not live in any dwelling where blood might have been spilled. He and Emma had gone to the count after the service in the Church of the Holy Sepulchre. They had confessed their deception to him and received his forgiveness and blessing. They had been wed not long afterward.

This day, Emma was digging in a small plot of earth outside the front door. She was planting vegetables. A scarf covered her hair, and she reached up now and then to push a stray lock out of her eyes.

Theo had just returned from the morning council. Jerusalem had been restored to order, but there was still much to do. He had been given the task of clearing the sand-filled wells outside the city. It was hard, hot, tedious labor, and his wound still gave him trouble, but the work suited him well. He toiled beside the men assigned to help him from sun-up to sundown, grateful for the opportunity to tire himself to the point where he could not think. There were many things he did not want to think about. After the battle, he and Emma had turned to each other in desperation. Neither of them could sleep. Nor could they talk; there were no words for the guilt and horror that haunted them. Each night, they had held each other wordlessly during the long black hours until the dawn.

At first, Emma had dug in the garden soil with a kind of frenzied fury. Gradually, however, as she created order and beauty out of the wild bramble that had been there before, she calmed. Her hands shaped the earth with more tenderness. Theo brought water every evening and they rationed it out carefully onto the long, straight rows she had created, nourishing the life that lay hidden in the buried seeds. Finally, she and Theo could sleep. They found words to say to each other. They could comfort each other with their love. As the days went by, life slowly became bearable again.

Now, as he watched her, Theo felt a hollowness within him being filled. Flowers bloomed in their garden, as if in defiance of the red-earthed desolation of the hills around them. Thick-leaved trees gave shade. In one of them, the song of a solitary bird trilled out clear and pure. Emma looked up just then and met his gaze. She smiled—a small, tentative smile. Theo's heart leaped. It was the first time she had smiled since the taking of Jerusalem.

A hail from the gate startled them. Amalric leaped over the low stone wall and loped over to sit beside Theo.

"Good morrow, Emma," he called. "Your garden does marvelously well."

Emma straightened up and brushed off her skirt.

"And a good morrow to you, Amalric," she called back. She disappeared into the house, but reappeared almost immediately carrying a bowl of oranges the color of sunshine itself and a flagon of wine. She brought them over and placed them on a low table beside Theo and Amalric, then seated herself.

"You heard, Theo, this morning—Duke Godfrey steadfastly refuses to allow himself to be crowned king of Jerusalem," Amalric said, picking up one of the golden fruits and tossing it from hand to hand. "He will allow himself only the title 'Defender of the Holy Sepulchre.'"

"Duke Godfrey is an honorable man," Theo replied. "He is as honorable in peace as he was in war."

"*Was* in war?" Amalric exclaimed. "So you believe our fighting days are over now?"

"We have won Jerusalem," Emma said. "We have given the Holy Lands back to the Church. What more is there to do?"

"What more, indeed?" Amalric asked. "So we will grow old and fat in peaceful governing of this land and city?"

Theo looked at him. "What more do you want, my friend?" he asked.

Amalric jumped to his feet. "Something! I know not what, but something!" He began to stride back and forth across the narrow garden. "This suits you, Theo, I can see that. You are growing brown and contented. I am pleased for you. But this peace that you enjoy so much is suffocating me. I am dying here!"

"Peace bores you?" Emma asked.

"It does. I need the excitement of battle, the sound of trumpets to send the blood coursing through my veins."

"And the killing? It bothers you not?" Emma asked.

"Killing is part of war. I accept it."

"Perhaps you need it."

Amalric looked at Theo sharply. "What do you mean by that?" he demanded, his voice suddenly harsh.

"Nothing. I am sorry. Please, forget my words, I spoke nonsense." Theo rose and placed his hand on Amalric's arm.

"What will you do?" Emma asked.

Amalric turned to her, and his eyes brightened again. "I have asked my lord Godfrey if I can return to Bouillon. There are still battles to be fought. I could be useful there."

"You would leave us? You would leave Jerusalem?" Theo stared at him.

"I would, my friend. And I would tempt you to come with me if I could, but I fear that would be impossible." He looked over at Emma and laughed, then tossed her the orange.

She caught it and held it carefully, as if it were something very precious.

† † †

"Would you go with him?" Emma asked that night as they lay entwined on their cot, the room lit only by the lambent glow of the last embers of their fire. "If it were not for me, would you go with him?"

"No," Theo answered, "I would not. I will miss Amalric when he goes. He has been my constant companion and true friend for the last three years. We have fought together and saved each other's life more times than I can count, but I would not go with him."

"Why not?"

The clash of weapons echoed in Theo's memory. The noises and the smells of war. The eyes of every man he had ever killed. He held Emma even more tightly.

"I could not," he said. "I am not like Amalric. If that means I am less of a man, then so be it. But I, too, have had my war. All I pray for now is that this peace that torments Amalric so should continue. I want not my children to know war."

He looked beyond Emma to where his sword stood propped in the shadows. The iron blade was twisted and notched. He had not yet asked the blacksmith to repair it.

He knew then he never would.

KARLEEN BRADFORD is one of Canada's
most respected young adult authors. She is
the author of several historical and contem-
porary stories, including *Windward Island*,
which won the 1990 Max and Greta Ebel
Award, *There Will Be Wolves*, winner of the
1993 Canadian Library Association Young
Adult Book Award, and the recently published
Thirteenth Child.

Having lived in cities all over the world, Karleen
Bradford now lives in Owen Sound, Ontario.